Amaryllis

Amaryllis

Craig Crist-Evans

CANDLEWICK PRESS
CAMBRIDGE, MASSACHUSETTS

Copyright © 2003 by Craig Crist-Evans

First paperback edition 2006

The Library of Congress has cataloged the hardcover edition as follows:

Crist-Evans, Craig
Amaryllis / Craig Crist-Evans.
p.   cm.
Summary: Jimmy and his older brother Frank share a love of surfing and their problems with a drunken father, until Frank turns eighteen and goes to Vietnam.
ISBN 0-7636-1863-2 (hardcover)
[1. Brothers—Fiction. 2. Fathers and sons—Fiction.
3. Vietnamese Conflict, 1961–1975—Fiction.
4. Florida—Fiction.] I. Title.

PZ7.C869635 Am 2003
[Fic]—dc21   2002034997

ISBN 0-7636-2990-1 (paperback)

2   4   6   8   10   9   7   5   3   1

Printed in the United States of America

This book was typeset in Sabon.

Candlewick Press
2067 Massachusetts Avenue
Cambridge, Massachusetts 02140

visit us at www.candlewick.com

for Kita . . .

My deep appreciation to Marion Dane Bauer, Ann Cardinal, Bonnie Christensen, Yann Crist-Evans, David Daboll, Greg Dunkling, Guadalupe Farias, Jack Gantos, Greg Grange, Krista Groshong, Lee Bennett Hopkins, Marie Lemonier, Bobbi Miller, Sylvaine Montaudouin, David Patterson, Graham Salisbury, Anita Silvey, Alice Soule-Collins, Donna Stone, retired U.S. Army Gen. Russell Todd, and Roger Weingarten. Special thanks to Linda Pratt for her faith and guidance. And finally, my gratitude with a touch of pure amazement to Kara LaReau for careful reading and the most exhaustive editorial comments I've ever seen. Without the encouragement and help of these friends and colleagues, this book would not be.

PROLOGUE

The first time I waded into the Atlantic, Frank was there beside me, holding my hand. It was April. I had just turned six. Frank would have been nine. Mom and Dad had taken us out of school and, loaded into Mom's green Rambler station wagon, off we went for a vacation in Florida, one big happy family. Three days on the road, driving little country roads through the South, and when we stopped, we stopped at the ocean. I remember being afraid of the water because I couldn't see the other side. But Frank was brave. He always was.

On the first night out we stayed in a motel in a small town in West Virginia. When we got up the next morning, we discovered the whole town preparing for a festival. By the time we finished breakfast, people were in the streets square dancing and climbing greased poles to win a pig and screaming at teams of men doing fire-hose races. They were all dressed in western clothes—cowboy hats and boots, and those little string ties with turquoise medallions pulled up to their throats.

"Come on, boys," Dad said. "Let's go."

Frank sat on the bed with his arms crossed on his chest, his eyes squinched together.

"I don't want to."

"Excuse me?" Dad asked angrily.

"I want to stay here and watch TV."

"We're all going," Dad said with finality, his voice sharp and hard like the edge of a knife.

I dug through my suitcase and pulled out my jeans, cowboy holster, and cap gun, and went out to the car to find my hat. When I came back into the motel room, I was dressed and ready to go out in the streets and dance with all the hillbillies, as Dad called them.

"Put your shorts on," he said.

"But, Dad, I want to be a cowboy."

"Get your shorts on *now*," he shot back. "We're on vacation. You wear shorts on vacation. You are *not* going to look like a hillbilly."

It didn't make any sense to me, but I couldn't argue with him. Mom came in and saw what was happening. She found my shorts in a suitcase and winked at me. It was the normal, everyday, conspiratorial wink that said, *You and I know better, but let's not make him mad.*

Frank got up off the bed, glaring at both of them, and sullenly headed for the door.

"Just let him wear his cowboy stuff," he said, the door banging shut behind him.

"That's enough out of you," Dad growled after him.

For the next couple of days I felt like something had been sucked out of our vacation. I went from looking forward to a week in Florida to feeling a vague dread about the whole thing. I remember asking Frank if he thought Mom and Dad were taking us there to leave us on a beach somewhere. I've always had a flair for melodrama, but it seemed like a possibility. Frank just shrugged, a gesture he'd perfected that meant *Don't ask me, Yes,* and *Who cares?*, all at the same time.

"What would it matter?" he said, shrugging again.

The whole trip was one of Dad's grand schemes to build family unity. At least that's what he said. The funny thing is that each time he dreamed up some great vacation, it didn't have anything to do with the rest of us. This time, he wanted to check Florida out and look around for a job. It would be years before we knew that his job in Ohio had been falling apart, that we had to move somewhere, and that in Dad's typical style when things weren't going his way, the farther the better.

When we got to Cocoa Beach, we found a motel right next to the ocean and things started looking up. Dad unpacked the car, then Mom made sandwiches and we ate lunch. All I could think about was getting in the water. Frank and I finished the sandwiches and started to run toward the waves, but Dad called us back.

"Sit tight," he said. "You've got to digest your lunch first."

After the obligatory hour's wait, we raced down the beach and Frank went splashing in.

"Come on, Jimmy," he shouted, waving his hands over his head. "Come on in."

I was frozen, my feet sinking into the wet sand at the edge of the water.

"Come on in!" he shouted again.

"I can't," I whispered, feeling miserable and small.

Frank looked at me for a minute, then paddled back to shore and walked up to where I was standing.

"What's wrong, Jimmy?"

"It's so big," I said. "What if I get lost?"

He laughed.

"You won't get lost," he reassured me. "I'll be right beside you."

He took my hand and I marched stiffly beside my brother into the Atlantic Ocean. It was cool, and the sharp sting of the salt in my eyes surprised me. Pretty soon, I was bouncing in the small waves and splashing Frank when he came near. We played all afternoon, then reluctantly came in and showered so we could go to the motel restaurant to eat.

After dinner, Frank and I were sitting on the concrete curb surrounding an old shuffleboard court, kicking sand and seashells, when Dad came outside and sat down with us. The sky had grown dark and stars were popping out. The sound of waves—small ones, barely formed and lazily rolling toward the beach—was something I had never heard before. It was the first time I realized that the whole world wasn't like Ohio.

"Dad, listen," I said. "Doesn't it sound like wind in the trees?"

"Yes," he whispered, "it does."

We sat there for a long time, listening to the waves. A little later, Mom came out and stretched out in a chaise lounge. She started singing hymns from church and we all joined in. At one point, Dad laughed and said something about this being the best church he'd ever been in. I pulled my knees up to my chest with my arms, a warm feeling rushing around in me that I didn't want to lose. Of all the things I remember about our family, this was one of the times I thought maybe we could be normal after all.

By now the sky was pitch-black and the stars were like a million pinpricks blinking everywhere. Dad stood up and stretched.

"Let's swim," he said.

A kind of excitement bubbled up in the back of my throat and my heart started beating fast as I ran back to the room and pulled on my still-wet swim trunks. Frank was a little bit ahead of me as we raced Dad down to the water. I wasn't scared until I felt the cool water swirling around my feet and sucking the sand out from under me. Frank must have noticed my hesitation; he came over and took my hand, and together we waded out to where the water rose above our knees.

"I was OK," I protested. "I didn't need any help."

"I know," he said.

Dad was already in the water, floating on his back. In the dark, in silhouette, he looked like a giant sea monster floating there. He paddled up to where Frank and I were standing and spit a plume of water straight up in the air. I splashed him and then Frank too. When I swished my hand through the water, pale ribbons of light trailed after it.

"Frank," I said, "look."

And Frank dragged his hand too, making long, curvy shapes and circles.

Dad came over and stood above us. The moon had risen just above the horizon, and in the light I could see his face. It looked soft, as if the lines and hard edges had washed away in the sea. "What do you think it is?" he asked.

"I think it's something in our skin that washes off and lights up in the water," Frank offered.

"I think it's magic," I said.

"You're right," said Dad. "It is magic."

Chapter 1

September 28, 1967
Da Nang

Hey Jimmy,

You wouldn't believe the jungle here—trees so thick you almost have to squeeze between them. And everything is sort of glazed with a soft green light. At night, after the moon comes up, the monkeys start to chatter high up in the branches. Then the birds chime in. Then insects. And there's this lizard that sounds like he's yelling fuck you *from somewhere far off in the jungle. If you think about the nights we camped out in the Everglades, it's like that, only ten times louder.*

And it's always wet. If it's not raining, then you're sweating so much even your socks are soaked. It gets so bad, my buddy Tom—he's from Georgia—got some kind of rash on his feet and can't walk ten steps without screaming.

After boot camp, Jimmy, I thought anything was freedom, but the way they stuffed us in the transport, then slammed the doors . . . I've never felt so far from home. Before we even got off the ground. But still, it's good to be this far from the old man.

Anyway, we landed at Da Nang and hung at the base for three days before they sent us out. It isn't really all that bad. In country. *That's what they say here for being in Nam—in country. Hot. Wet. I know you don't care about this, but everything they say about the weed over here is true. My first night in, a bunch of us rolled one up and smoked, and I hardly remember anything from then until we got orders to move out last week.*

Here, in camp, it's been two days soft and three days out. Out is in the jungle, the mountains. Sometimes we find tunnels and we throw so damn much juice down in them you could melt the North Pole in a heartbeat. I haven't seen any gooks yet. Gooks, VC, the Cong, Charlie. It's funny how we've got so many names for the enemy. It's almost cozy, like we're hunting our best friends down for dinner.

I suppose the news looks like it did when I was there. The World looks a long way off from here. But so far it's not awful. I've got a couple buddies. Good pot. The days we lay around the camp are fine. If I close my eyes sometimes I think I'm back in Florida.

Frank

⋀

My brother Frank's eighteen. Just turned last March. He always said he'd do anything to get out of this house. But join the army and go to Vietnam? Don't get me wrong. It's not that I think he's stupid for signing up; it's just that I worry. I mean, watch the news. Villages getting napalmed, Vietcong crawling through the jungle, lying in wait, then pouncing in the middle of the night. At the end of every segment, Walter Cronkite lists the body count. It usually sounds pretty good for us, but there are always body bags with American flags draped over them getting loaded into cargo planes.

Dad doesn't say much about it, and it makes me wonder if he secretly hopes Frank gets killed. I know parents aren't supposed to think that way about their kids, but my dad is a case. When Frank was still around, some-times they'd yell so loud the neighbors would call my mom and ask her to make them stop. Sometimes she'd stand there, her hair pulled back tight, arms crossed over her chest, and watch them, knowing there was nothing at all she could say that would end it. She always got a look on her face that seemed to say, *I didn't ask for this. Please let there be peace in this house.* Sloopy, our basset hound, got into it too. After a couple of rounds of escalating voices, she'd chime in, howling like the moon was coming up in our own backyard.

I've never figured out why Dad hated Frank so much. Maybe because Frank was not afraid of him. Maybe it's just that everything about Frank confused Dad. Frank was smart and able to talk really well. I know it sounds funny, but my brother is a philosopher. The two of them would get into an argument and Frank would almost always make his point in a way that Dad couldn't argue with, so Dad would smack him or ground him for a week instead. Actually, I think it's more that in Frank, Dad saw all the things he could have been if he hadn't gotten married so young and had all of us to take care of, as if he both envied and resented Frank at the same time.

I don't want to paint a completely awful picture. My dad has his good moments. Last week, he took me to the beach and sat in the sand for two hours while I paddled out and waited for the lines of big swells to turn into waves. When I came in, soaked to the bones, as he would say, and burnt from the salt and the sun, we jumped in the car and headed back along A1A.

Singer Island is not the greatest place to surf. It's not the greatest place to drive either, but Dad seemed calm and happy as we passed the hotels and tennis clubs, the rows of houses, the little artificial jungles of palmetto, sable palm, and sea grape.

We had just passed the *Amaryllis* when, out of the blue, Dad asked, "Do you miss your brother?"

He sounded choked up, and that surprised me. I wanted to tell him that it scared me, that Frank was who I talked to when things were bad, that I couldn't imagine my brother lugging an M-16 into some swampy distance with a bunch of other boys his age who were probably all just fresh from "the World," as Frank has come to refer to every place except the war.

"I don't think about it much," I said.

Dad turned his head to look at me.

"Oh," he said.

We drove the rest of the way home in silence.

We turned left and crossed the Intracoastal Waterway. Along the rails of the bridge, a bunch of men and women stood, casting heavy lures and chunks of raw bait over the side and then reeling slowly. One man, fat enough to take two seats on a Greyhound bus, was sweating and tugging hard against his rod, bent almost double as he tried to bring in a big one.

Mom was in the kitchen when we got back.

"What have my boys been up to?" she said as I walked around the corner from the living room. She was bending over a large pot of something boiling on the stove, her hair tucked back behind one ear.

"Surfing!" Dad's voice boomed from the carport, as if he'd been hanging ten and tucking for some imaginary pipeline himself.

I've got mixed feelings about having him take me to the beach. On the one hand, I like to think we've got a normal relationship, that I can do things with my dad. On the other, it's just plain embarrassing to have him waiting on the dunes and then ranting about what fun we had. I mean, he sits there in his bright yellow windbreaker and those goofy sunglasses staring at the girls. I push out as far as I can go and watch the waves. I can't wait till next month when I get my license and can drive myself to the beach.

"Beef stew and succotash," my mother said, bending over me, "your favorite."

Where she gets these ideas, I don't know. Depending on when you ask, she'll tell you my "favorite" is meatloaf, broiled grouper, banana bread and peanut butter, or Cheerios with raisins and buttermilk. She doesn't have a clue. The truth is, I like just about anything, especially after being in the water all day.

⟋⟍

As I was saying, Dad has his good moments. But he has his bad ones too. Usually, they have something to do with whiskey. That night, I was really beat. All day in the sun. Some terrific sets rolling in all afternoon. A big dinner under my belt. All I wanted to do was pull off my shoes, curl up on the couch, and watch TV. But Dad had other ideas.

"Time to wash the dishes!" he hollered from the kitchen.

"I did them all last week," I hollered back, sinking into the fat cushions on the couch.

"Young man," he started, "I don't like the tone of your voice. I keep a roof over your head and food in your belly. I even sacrifice my Saturdays to take you to the beach. It's high time you took *your* responsibilities in this household seriously."

He came around the corner with a glass in his hand. The whiskey sloshed as he swung his arm to point at me, and then he realized he was spilling his drink. He took a sip and glared.

"Get your ass in there this minute and do those

dishes," he growled. "You're not watching the god-damned tube until they're clean and dry."

At least when Frank was around, we split the chores, or when I was stuck doing something rank, he'd at least be there to give me a hard time and make me laugh. Now it's just me. I'm beginning to understand why Frank wanted out of here so bad and why, when he got the chance, he had to go.

Frank would have told Dad to shove it, and the rest of the night would have been a shouting match. I pulled my shoes back on and slumped across the terrazzo floor. Mom had stacked everything next to the sink, then gone out back to sit in one of the lawn chairs by the bougainvillea. I could hear her singing quietly, some church hymn I could almost remember.

Chapter 2

October 15, 1967
Da Nang

Hey Jimmy,

Did you think I forgot you? I promise, I'll try to write as often as I can, no matter how tough it gets over here. Just like when we sat up all those nights at home and talked, I need to tell someone about this place . . . and tag, you're it.

Truth is, I miss those talks. No one here understands when I want to talk about the way a wave will lift you into some incredible state of ecstasy, push you toward the beach, then drop you gently like some giant's hand, then you jump off the board and walk like a king back up to where the girls are watching. But you do. For a kid brother, you're pretty damned smart. Probably just rubbed off from hanging around with me.

You asked in your last letter what patrol is like. Well, it's not the Boy Scouts. They send you out with a week's rations and after that you've got to fend for yourself. If we're lucky, we run across a village and pray the gooks are cool. We try to ask, but mostly we just take whatever we can find. The lieutenant sometimes swings his gun around and makes a lot of noise. We know he's only putting on a show, but it scares the hell out of the villagers and they cough up grub.

If we're not so lucky, stuck out in the jungle with nothing like a hut in sight, we have to eat what we can find. One of the guys trapped a rat last week and roasted it in camp. I couldn't eat it. Instead, I smoked some reefer with Tom and we sat at the perimeter listening to the frogs and some weird bird off in the trees.

So far, we haven't seen the enemy. I hear things in the night and can't get back to sleep, but I think I'm just nervous. The other guys, the ones who've been here for a while, sleep like babies. Remember when we used to camp out in the woods, the way the cypress trees would scrape *together in the middle of the night? Remember how I'd tell you it was ghosts? Well, here the ghosts are real.*

Frank

PS: Got a girlfriend yet, Romeo?

I hate it when Frank teases me about girls. He always had it made. All he had to do was walk down the hallway at school and they'd fall all over him. Me, they don't even notice. But I'm not like Frank. Though I'm not bad-looking, I'm short for my age and I'm pretty quiet. It's not that I don't care about girls: I *do*. But I almost never get a chance to talk to them.

Sometimes, I think my family is so weird no girl will come near me. And then I wonder if it would help to have a girlfriend, a friend to talk to, somebody who understands how screwy it is for me at home. Someone who knows but tells me it's OK. Frank had Susan, and I know she helped him, at least for a while.

One night, Frank grabbed me and told me we were going for a ride. I thought we were going out to see his friends. He sometimes took me along and tried to get me to smoke pot with him. But that's another story.

This time, we drove down to Lake Park and pulled up

in front of Susan's house. The sun was starting to fade into sheets of red gauze above the trees and roofs. A dog down the street was barking like the devil himself was trying to steal his bowl of crunchies.

I could make out the shape of a '57 Ford up on blocks to the side of the house. The yard was thick with palms and orange trees. Frank got out of the car without answering my questions about what we were up to. He walked to the front door and banged. Next thing I know, Susan comes out followed by the goofiest-looking girl I've ever seen.

"Hi," she said, when they got back to the car, "I'm Trina, Susan's sister."

She was wearing jeans and a tee shirt, both smudged pretty much all over with grease that had been washed and dried into the fabric so much it was permanent. She smelled like gasoline.

"Hi, Jimmy," Susan piped. And then: "This'll be fun!"

"Hey, Joon," said Frank, his variation on what my dad called me, "I thought we'd catch a movie at the Southside."

He was smiling, pleased with himself. He looked at me, and then he looked at Trina, then back at me.

"Yeah," I managed. "That'll be great."

Susan disengaged from Frank, who had put his arm around her shoulders.

"Didn't you tell him?" she asked.

"I wanted to surprise him."

I was surprised, all right. I think Frank was laughing all the way to the drive-in, but it was quiet and to himself.

The movie was *Nevada Smith,* where Steve McQueen goes after three men who killed his mother and father and executes them one by one. Up front, Frank and Susan were necking. In the back seat, Trina kept to herself and leaned against the door, listening to the tinny voices coming from the speaker, which was hooked to the passenger window up front.

Smith (McQueen) had gotten himself thrown into prison just so he could get his hands on the second of his victims. He had hatched an elaborate plot to befriend the guy and escape with him, just so he could kill him. I don't always get absorbed in movies, but this was cool. The men in the prison, which was plunked down right in the middle of a swamp, were finally allowed to relax. The guards brought in a bunch of women from a plantation down the river, and each man hooked up with one of the women and headed back to the prison barracks. At fifteen, this was about as close as I'd ever gotten to sex, and I was paying attention.

"I fix cars," Trina said, matter-of-fact, as if I'd just asked her what the one thing is that she does to make a mark in the universe.

"Yeah," I said, not taking my eyes off the screen,

where by now Smith was about to put the moves on this beautiful raven-haired woman.

"Yeah," she comes back, "I've got an old Ford I'm working on right now. The engine runs, but she burns oil and I have to change the rings. My dad helps me, but I do most of the work myself."

I was hoping Frank or Susan would tell her to shut up, but their heads had by now sunk below the edge of the front seat and they couldn't care less if Steve McQueen was about to get lucky or make his slick escape plans.

"Have you ever taken down a straight six?" she asked me, edging closer on the seat.

I realized she had decided enough was enough and she was going to get my attention, impress and seduce me with car talk. I fixed my eyes on the screen, but Smith was now outside in the shadows, talking earnestly to the girl about getting a boat. If they had worked up a sweat inside, I missed it. Trina didn't seem to care that she was interrupting a perfectly good movie with her talk about drive trains and universal joints. Frank and Susan were lost in their own version of the prison-camp shuffle, making sounds that reminded me of the washing machine working on a particularly heavy load of laundry.

Finally, I turned to ask her to be quiet so I could

watch the rest of the movie, and I found myself staring right into her eyes. Her glasses, actually. She had skootched all the way over to my side of the car and turned her face toward me, eyes closed, mouth puckered up. I didn't know what to do, so I sat there frozen while she moved in for the kill, planting her lips sloppily against mine and moving her face around like you see in old Bogart movies. She didn't try to slip me the tongue and I didn't invite it. I guess it could have been worse.

By the time she started talking about cars again, Smith was riding out with a bunch of outlaws, his third victim firmly in his scripted sights, and I'd completely missed what happened to the guy in the prison camp. Later, driving home, Trina sat against me, smiling. I had my arm draped around her shoulder out of necessity; there was no place else to put it. I couldn't wait to get the girls out of the car so I could strangle Frank. We drove along Federal Highway past Carvel and Dunkin' Donuts and a thousand junk shops. Two cops were parked on stools in the Dunkin' Donuts, both of them bent over coffee. The waitress, who was probably a year older than me, was filling up their cups. For a second, I panicked, thinking if Frank pulled in right now, the cops could arrest me for the murderous thoughts I had about my brother.

Now Frank is sleeping in a jungle, nine thousand miles from a bad blind date at a drive-in theater. I never called Trina after our fateful, awful make-out, but right now, I'd talk to her just because she was part of something I remember about Frank.

I read the letter again before I go to bed, the desk lamp bright on the yellow paper, his lousy handwriting jumping from the page as loud as a voice.

In the living room, I can hear my father talking on the phone. Mom is out back, sitting in the lawn chair, getting a moon tan, as my father calls it. I get a sheet of paper out of my desk and sit down to write. *Dear Frank* . . . but I am tired and don't have much to say. It's hard to tell him about school or Mom or Dad. I want to sneak next door, into his room, and sit cross-legged on the floor and tell him everything. How hard it is to be alone.

I put the paper away and turn off the light. It's funny how much we talked when he was here and how hard it is to write now that he's gone. There's a hurricane brewing, and before I drift off to sleep, I think about the waves along the beach at Singer, punching hard against the shore as the wind comes up.

Chapter 3

October 20, 1967
Da Nang

Jimmy,

My buddy Tom got shot. He'll live, but I've never seen a thing so scary. Right through the chest. We were standing in a canebrake along an irrigation ditch, rice paddies stretching like silver sheets toward the horizon. There was nothing out there. Nothing. All of a sudden, bullets started flying and the Cong rose up like ghosts from the water. Tom was crouched in front of me, taking compass readings. "East," he said. "We're heading east." Then he stood up fast, like someone grabbed him by the shirt and tugged. He looked at me and smiled. Can you imagine that? He smiled. And then, like it was slow motion, he brought his hand up to his chest and sat back down, blood seeping between his fingers.

I don't know how long the fight went on. They shot. We shot. Branches of trees snapped off, the canebrake came apart like somebody was mowing. And then, as suddenly as it started, it was over. The gooks disappeared.

The medic was pinned down and couldn't get to Tom while we were firing, but when the bullets stopped, he ran across the open ground, tall grass waving all around his shoulders, put some bandages against the wound, and pressed. The guns were silent, but my heart was pounding like some mad drum, and the sun glittered on the rice paddies like nothing had happened.

I had to keep the pressure on while the medic fumbled through his bag for morphine. It seemed like hours, but finally the choppers came. Last thing Tom said to me before they evac'd him was, "Damn it, Frank, we're heading in the wrong direction."

Jimmy, I can't tell you how bad it gets. Sometimes I get really scared; it's funny when it comes. I wasn't scared when the Cong were shooting at *us, but after, when Tom was crumpled like a piece of wadded-up paper on the ground, a cold flush came over me that felt like the biggest wave of winter rolling in, pushing me to the bottom.*

We've been back on base two days and things are starting to mellow out. It's so strange to be out there, in the jungle, spooked at every step, every sound, and then back here on base with the Doors on the sound system, some GI rolling joints, and a cold six-pack of Budweiser inside the tent. I get to go to Saigon on leave next month. The Paris of the Orient. I guess it's really like the World . . . cars, nightclubs, girls. Well, I'll think about all that later. For now, it's me, signing off from Nam.

Frank

Sometimes in the middle of the night I wake up thinking Frank is here, in the next room, sleeping. Like that phantom limb thing I've read about, where you still feel your leg, even after it's been amputated. Tonight, I'm so sure he's here, I get up and go into his room and stand there in the moonlight. The room smells empty, even though Frank's stuff is exactly the way he left it. His bed, his Doors poster, the quote from e. e. cummings that says *damn everything but the circus,* the model boats he built and set up like armadas on his dresser. I don't know how long I stand here, breathing quietly, imagining a conversation with my brother. All I know is that I miss him bad.

Outside, the wind is picking up. The weatherman says Hurricane Jesse will make landfall Friday night, somewhere near Miami.

⋏

Our first year in Florida, when Hurricane Betsy hit, I thought the world was coming to an end. It was my first hurricane. We didn't have a clue as to what to expect. For days, we stacked canned fruit and beans and boxes of dry milk and bottled water on the kitchen shelves; we stocked up on candles, batteries, and playing cards.

The night before Betsy hit—this was September, 1965—my mother rounded us up—Dad, Frank, and me—and gave us The Lecture. She had been reading up on hurricanes, and we were going to do everything according to The Plan. She handed sheets of paper to each of us and began to talk in a slow, national-park-service-ranger voice.

"Jim," she said to my dad, "you have to board the windows up. Jalousies blow out like popcorn in a good one. Frank, you fill the tub with water in case we're stranded. Jimmy, I want you to set out candles in all the rooms so we can find them quickly if the power goes out. And remember" she said sternly, looking straight at me, "I don't want anyone going outside until it blows over."

Betsy hit land at two the next afternoon, Thursday, September 9, 1965. By three everything was black, and sheets of rain pounded the ground. A river formed in the street, rushing toward Lake Worth, which is really the Intracoastal Waterway. The wind was so loud I couldn't hear the radio unless I put my ear right up to it. A voice kept repeating the same things: how fast the wind was blowing (135 miles per hour), when the eye of the storm would be over us (ten the next morning), and how long it would take to get things back to normal (a week). I listened. I wanted details, stories of people picked up and blown across the county, pictures on the evening news of pieces of straw pounded like nails into palm trees, cars floating through the streets of West Palm Beach.

That night, we played gin rummy. The radio kept up its monotonous reports of flooded roads, National Guard assistance, and how hard the governor was working to make sure communications didn't break down. By ten, when none of the walls had been blown in and none of the jalousie windows had burst like land mines, we went to bed. I was disappointed. I wanted disaster. Instead, the wind hummed steadily outside my room, dragging me into sleep.

I woke with a start the next morning. I had dreamed the ocean climbed across Lake Worth, all the way to our house. I could step out the front door and climb onboard a ship that was something like the Ark, loaded with animals and families with their cars, and Frank— somehow the captain of the boat—was ushering everyone aboard with a graceful bow and a handshake. I remember jumping up and looking at the floor to make sure it wasn't flooded. When I was sure the water hadn't yet made it into the house, I stood on my bed and looked outside.

The wind was still howling; pieces of grass and seaweed flew by as if someone were throwing them. A coconut bounced down the street. Piles of trash and broken branches clogged the gutters everywhere and occasional cars sloshed along like barges, drivers hunched over the steering wheels, windshield wipers going full blast.

"Jimmy! Frank!" my mother hollered from the kitchen. "Breakfast is ready."

To my mother's way of thinking, you are at the breakfast table when breakfast is ready, no matter what else you might have to do. Even in the face of imminent disaster, there has to be a sort of order to everything. It was seven o'clock in the morning. School was out for at least the next three days, because it was Labor Day weekend—not to mention there was a hurricane blowing—and Mom had breakfast ready in time for all the schedules we didn't have to keep.

"I don't know why you boys can never be ready on time," she said as we came around the corner to the kitchen table. Dad was already seated, his head cradled in his hands.

"I've got a headache," he said.

"Mom," Frank said, "there's a hurricane outside, we don't have school, and we were sound asleep ten minutes ago."

"Don't talk to your mother that way!" Dad snapped, rubbing his forehead.

There was a roughness in his voice that meant today was probably not going to be a good day. He reached for the bacon, which was already starting to firm up in its bed of pig fat spread out on a paper towel.

"I was simply pointing out the illogic in racing around to get ready for something we aren't going to do," Frank said.

"Maybe you should let your mother and me worry about that." Dad was smoldering now.

"Why can't anyone in this household except you question anything?" Frank said. His voice was low, kind of like the air outside, a hurricane brewing but not quite a storm yet.

"Excuse me?" Dad pushed his chair back.

This was always his response when one of us questioned him. *Excuse me.* As if we had made a mistake and he was giving us a chance to rephrase.

"You know, Jimmy and I have the right to say things too," Frank continued.

"Your mother has been up since six, cooking and getting ready. Show some respect," Dad barked.

"There's a goddamned hurricane stirring up out there!" Frank exclaimed. "I could have done without eggs at seven A.M."

"Do you pay the bills? Do you work your ass off every day to keep a roof over our heads? I'm tired of you arguing with everything I say."

Dad had stabbed a piece of bacon but had stopped midsentence, the limp meat hanging from his fork, grease dripping slowly onto the tablecloth.

"You're dripping," Frank said, and pushed himself away from the table.

"Where do you think you're going?"

"I'm going to get ready and wait for the bus. It should be along in a couple of days. Once the storm blows over."

I ate quickly, and while everyone else was busy debating the fine points of the appropriate way to be a smartass with one's parents, I slipped outside. At the back of the carport, I pried open the doors to the utility shed where we kept the lawnmower, rakes and shovels, bicycles, and my skateboard. I'd only made the skateboard a week before, when a friend had shown me how he'd taken the wheels off a pair of steel skates he didn't use anymore and screwed them to the bottom of a board he'd cut about eighteen inches long.

I had to wade through part of the yard to get to the sidewalk. The wind howled and I could see pieces of wood, branches, palm fronds, and Coke cans all blowing and skittering across the street. The sidewalk wasn't dry, but it was not underwater. I put the board down and placed my right foot on it, pushing at the same time with my left foot. I rolled along easily for a few feet and then swung my left foot down and pushed again. Rain pelted my face, making me squint hard. I pushed off with one foot and rolled, pushed off and rolled.

It took forever, but I made it down to Lake Worth. Big Australian pines were bent nearly double. The rocks along the shore had completely disappeared beneath the rising water. Dead fish and seaweed lay scattered everywhere. A traffic light swung wildly from its wire overhead, blinking red, red, red.

I sat down on a soggy stone at the corner of the Rutlands' yard at the end of the street and watched the waterway swell, whitecaps breaking up and over the seawall. The boats rocked and dove, tethered by thick ropes that looked like they would snap at any minute.

I thought about Frank and my dad, fighting over the stupidest things while the world raged outside.

I got up, put the board back down, turned around, and headed back home. This time, the wind was with me. I remembered watching sailboats out on the Atlantic, sails filled with wind, sleek hulls cutting fast across the water. I noticed that I didn't have to push as often with my left foot. Then I had a brilliant idea. I unbuttoned my shirt and pulled it out of my jeans. Holding the tails in each hand, I spread it out like a snail and let the wind grab it. A gust of wind came up, and suddenly I was flying, both feet planted firmly on the board. *Click, clack, click, clack, click.* The steel wheels sounded like a train as I raced along the sidewalk. I was going uphill like someone had strapped a jet engine to my back.

One block, then two, and when I came up to our house I kept on going. I could see my mother in the carport, waving frantically. She was yelling something, but I couldn't hear her. I felt like Superman, a human miracle of flight, a racecar driver at the salt flats in Utah. Nothing could stop me now. I'd break the land speed record, get my name in the *Guinness Book of World Records,* and retire before I ever started working. Dad would leave me alone about fishing and Frank would be proud of me.

I didn't see the palm tree. The wind had knocked it over and now it lay square across the sidewalk. I hit it full speed and went flying, this time without my skateboard. I remember thinking about those people in the news who get picked up in a hurricane or tornado and are deposited miles away from where they started. I was afraid, thinking of the long walk home in the middle of a storm. Before I could navigate the far corners of the county, however, I landed without a stitch of grace in the middle of the sidewalk, breaking my fall with both hands.

Mom was already running across the yard before I could sit up. I tried to lean on my right hand, but a lightning bolt of pain shot up my arm. She bent down and lifted me in one motion, hugging me to her tightly.

"Oh, son, are you OK?" she asked tremulously.

My hand was hanging at a funny angle, but it didn't hurt. I could feel it swelling as we walked back toward the house. Dad was standing in the carport when we got there, hands on both hips, a look of fire in his eyes. I thought I would have been better off if the hurricane had blown me up to Georgia, but before I could turn and run, he grabbed me, tugged me to him, and smacked me in the face.

"Goddamn it!" he yelled so close to my ear I could feel the heat of his breath. "You were *told* not to go out in this. How stupid are you? Don't you ever listen?"

By now, I had remembered my swollen wrists and felt tears coming up in my eyes. Dad swung me around, banging my left hand into the car, and I screamed.

"Wait, Jim," my mother said, "I think he's hurt."

And then I passed out.

Riding in the car to the hospital, my dad griped the whole way about having to go out on a day like this. I sat sullen and in pain in the back seat, looking out across the city blocks transformed into islands of garbage and broken trees. There was only one doctor on duty, but we got in pretty quickly. He seemed bored. My mother told him what happened, while my father sat in the waiting room, an evil look fixed firmly on his face. It turned out both wrists were broken, and it took a while to put plaster casts on them.

All the way back out to the car, Dad was dead silent, a sure sign of his own version of the hurricane brewing; he was just biding his time and would explode when we got home. I forced myself to think about other things. For instance, I couldn't wait to go back to school with casts on my arms. There's something romantic and tragic about a broken bone, and I figured I could get some girls to sign the casts. Maybe they'd feel sorry for me. But then, I wasn't sure I'd live long enough to impress my classmates.

When we got home, Dad grabbed me out of the car, and together we marched into the house. Frank was watching the tube.

"Hey, Joon," he said, "tough break."

He was smiling. I didn't feel much like smiling, but I

was glad to see him, and somehow just knowing he could laugh about it made me feel better.

"Wipe that smile off your face." Dad glared at Frank, then turned to me. "And you get to your room. Don't come out until you've thought about your stupid behavior," he said to me, pointing down the hall.

"Great," I muttered under my breath, sulking down the hall to my room.

"Excuse me?" he said.

"Nothing," I said, and closed the door behind me.

I sat on the edge of my bed for a long while, feeling pretty miserable. Gradually, I became aware of something odd. Something huge in the world had shifted. It was like some crazy movie where they flash from one scene to the next and it takes you a second to adjust; at first I couldn't figure out what had happened. Then it hit me. The wind had died. Everything was completely still. It was eerie.

Outside, the trees were standing up again. Rain was still falling, but not very hard. The sky seemed frozen. I remembered the radio announcer talking about the progress of the storm. It would all start up again in an hour or two, but right then, that minute, we were in the eye of the hurricane.

Chapter 4

October 25, 1967
Pleiku

Joon,

When you go out in this jungle at night, it's so dark sometimes you can't see your hands. You brush up against trees, feeling the ground with your foot, judging distance by the length of each step.

And then there are the tunnels. Charlie digs these things miles long. He uses them to hide people and food, and to get from one village to another. I haven't had to do it yet, but sometimes we get orders to go down in and check them out.

One guy from the unit, Todd, went in one last week. The entrance was almost grown over in weeds, but if you were really looking, you could see where the ground opened up right there. Anyway, Todd climbed down in and I handed him his rifle. He was gone in an instant, like the earth swallowed him up.

The rest of us crouched near the entrance, drinking water from our canteens and watching the bush for any movement. Steve lit a cigarette and passed it around. After what seemed like an hour, we heard a dull thud and the ground shook slightly. We knew what it was but didn't want to talk about it. An hour passed, then two, and finally we packed up and moved out, each of us thinking our own prayer for Todd.

We marched three more hours, until it was almost dark, stopped, pitched tents, and ate. It had been a long day and we were all ready to crash. Sometime in the middle of the night—I don't know what time it was—the perimeter patrol started screaming, and the whole camp was up. I was still cinching up my pants when I got to where the sergeant was motioning everyone back. Someone had a flashlight pointed off into the bush.

You know how people always stop when they

see an accident, and part of it is wanting to see what death looks like? Or how bad someone is hurt? Maybe you just want to be sure it's someone else, that you're safe and alive, but you've got to look. Well, I followed the beam of that light and there he was. Todd. Mangled beyond belief, chunks of flesh just missing, half of his face gone, his uniform ripped off. They'd dragged what was left of him out of the tunnel, followed us all day, then left him here where we had to find him.

The next morning, we dug a hole and carried his body over, lowered him down, and said our prayers again. The first time he went down into the ground, we were hopeful he'd come out smiling, laughing at how easy it was to go below the surface of this hell on earth, crawl around with nothing but your heartbeat, and come back up into the clean sunlight. This time it was something else, a statement about how useless all of this really is, how one minute someone you know is telling you about his sister, or his hot rod back in Des Moines, and the next minute he shows up in the middle of the night, dead and shredded at the edge of your camp, so far from anything that matters, you can't remember anymore how it feels to sleep and dream of girls, the moon, the quiet swoosh of waves washing into the beach at night

when you can't see anything, but you can see
everything for a thousand miles.

We moved out by seven, all of us looking hard
into the jungle, knowing the VC were there watch-
ing. By the time we came out, a week later, no one
talked about it. The silence of the jungle was
inside us, and everything we said was just a
breath of fear, a whisper of what happens, finally,
to all of us, and nobody wanted to admit it.

> *Your brother,*
> *Frank*

⌃

The day after my accident, Betsy had pretty much moved
on. It was still raging up the coast, but here things were
slowly getting back to normal. People came out into
their yards and picked up the trash that had blown or
floated there over the past two days. Up and down the
street, piles of palm fronds, sheets of plywood, bottles,
soggy wads of newspaper, broken bicycles, and shredded
pieces of clothing began to appear along the curbs. Dad
went out before work and looked around. He paced the
front yard like a general reviewing the aftermath of
some great battle, then circled around the side of the
house and into the backyard.

I watched him pulling on the broken branches of the

orange trees and kicking loose coconuts around like soccer balls. Part of the chainlink fence had crumpled where something had smashed into it before bellowing on. Dad looked sour, so I stayed inside.

He hadn't said another word to me about my broken wrists, but Frank came in and aped around like he had his arm in a sling.

"Come on," I said, "it's not funny."

He looked at me for a moment with a mock-serious expression on his face.

"It's not?"

He tried to open my closet with his "broken" arm and slid down the wall in failure. Then he tried to pick his nose. I started laughing.

"Okay, okay. So it's funny."

By now I was leaning back on the bed and Frank was hovering over me with his arm stretched out like a wing. He started prancing around the room squawking like a chicken. The door to the room slammed open and Dad stood there.

"What the hell do you think you're doing?" he shouted at Frank, who dropped his arms and glanced over at me.

No one said anything at all. After a minute, Dad sort of slouched.

"Damn it," he said. "I'm out there cleaning up this goddamn mess in the yard, and you boys are in here clowning around."

He turned and left the room.

I reached over and turned on the radio. The DJ was giving us the skinny on the damage caused by Betsy. Most of it was normal stuff—roofs blown off houses, cars floating down the Intracoastal, boats washed up along the shore.

"And in the night," he started, "a Greek banana freighter called the *Amaryllis* was blown off course and nosed into the beach on Singer Island. It's not going anywhere."

"Wow," said Frank. "A ship. Can you imagine that?"

We'd only been in Florida for a few months, but I'd read about the shipwrecks up and down the coast. Spanish galleons, Portuguese treasure ships, pirates—the idea of our own shipwreck was more than a little exciting.

Things calmed down by the end of the weekend. I got used to doing everything without my hands, Dad and Frank got the yard cleaned up, and Mom climbed up each afternoon, on a step stool that she dragged around the yard, to wash the jalousie windows. She also went from tree to tree, picking fruit that was damaged in the storm but was still edible. I wandered around watching everyone work, feeling pretty useless and sorry for myself.

School was another story. Broken wrists are good attention-getters. By Thursday everyone I knew had signed my casts. And since I couldn't use my hands very well, the teachers let me off the hook for class participation and homework. They called on me, but that was about it. I decided right then that I would break something two or three times a year.

The following Saturday morning dawned bright and hot. Any remaining traces of the storm seemed to burn away in the brilliant sun. I got up and tried to rub my eyes, forgetting for a minute the casts that hung there like rocks at the ends of my arms. I walked out to the family room, blinking.

Frank was lounging on the rattan sofa Mom had bought last month at a flea market.

"You want to go surfing?" he asked.

"Yeah, right."

I waved my plaster-cast arms at him.

"Don't be such a wimp, Jimmy. You can go along and hang out, anyway."

As we loaded up the car and Frank tied his board onto the roof, I was not as impressed with my condition as I had been in third-period math during the week. I wanted to be able to paddle out and feel the waves behind me too. I got into the car, feeling sorry for myself again. Frank got in, started the car, backed out of the driveway, and turned toward Federal.

It was a perfect fall day. The sun was hot, and when we crossed over to Singer Island I could see the ocean glitter like diamonds. Everything seemed so normal—the sweet, humid air, the sound of waves crashing, and the voices of little kids playing out by the tide line—but the bits and pieces left from storm damage were a shock. All along the beach, there were broken palm trees bent at weird angles, and huge chunks of the dunes had disappeared. A few hotels were boarded up, the foundations washed out or the insides so flooded it would take weeks to get them clean. One hotel looked perfectly normal from the road, but the whole backside—the part facing the Atlantic—was missing.

I guess it says something about people that they walk right back out into the world as if nothing had happened after a hurricane has ripped trees up, blown houses down, and stranded speedboats two blocks from the nearest water. I don't know if it means we're survivors or just nuts, but the highway this Saturday morning was jammed with cars moving slowly in both directions.

After we finally found a parking spot, Frank got his board off the homemade roof rack and started down toward the beach. I still felt pretty useless and walked along behind him kicking pieces of coral and driftwood that lay along the path that wound through the dune grass and down to the beach. Frank was only a couple hundred feet from the car when he stopped suddenly and just stood there, his board wedged under his right arm, a bag in which he carried wax and his wet suit in the other.

"Come on, Frank," I said. "The sand is hot. Get moving."

But he didn't budge. I came up beside him and pushed him with my plaster arms.

"Look," he said, pointing toward the ocean.

A few hundred yards away, looming at the water's edge like a beached whale, was a huge ship. The bow was shoved unnaturally into the sand, waves running along the hull like schools of fish. The stern stretched out forever. On the far side I could see a bunch of surfers grouped and waiting. Swells lifted them up and dropped them, and then the set they were waiting for started rolling in. What was weird was that there were almost never any good waves on this part of the beach. As I watched, the surfers got up one by one and moved like dancers on the slick, steep fronts of waves, cutting in and out, turning hard and rising back toward the crest, then turning again and slicing across the face.

Frank started running. I followed, but it was awkward with my arms stiff and heavy. By the time I caught up with him, he was pulling on his wet suit. I looked up at the ship. It rose like a mountain out of the water, the long curve of its bow hanging out over the beach like one of those carved women on old-time sailing ships.

"The *Amaryllis*," I said.

I don't know how long we stayed out there that day in the shadow of the wreck, or how many times we went back over the next two years before Frank left for Nam. For some reason, the way the ship disrupted the current along the shore created set after set of great waves. After my arms were better, and Frank let me paddle his board out occasionally, I rode some of the best waves I've ever ridden there by the *Amaryllis*.

It became a kind of symbol and battle cry. Each Saturday we'd get up, throw down a bowl of cereal, and Frank would look at me and say, in a voice just barely above a whisper, "*Amaryllis*." Then we'd load his car and drive the five miles to Singer Island, eager to be swallowed up and spit back out at the crest of the perfect wave.

Chapter 5

Jimmy,

No one moves when the platoon is pinned down under fire. It's sort of like the way we used to play hide-and-seek. Sometimes we know they're out there and we dig in quietly, making nests in the grass, curling up at the base of trees. Other times, something in the jungle snaps, birds get spooked and fly, the monkeys stop chattering, or one of us sees something move out of the corner of his eye. Then, where fifteen guys were walking along a narrow path, suddenly there's no one. In the time it takes to blink, we're buried in the land-scape.

Another guy bought it this week. We were on a reconnaissance mission near Pleiku, looking for a band of gooks that's been active in the villages. This guy and I had night duty. The moon was lifting up against the backdrop of trees and mountains. It was so quiet you could hear the water moving in an irrigation ditch beside our post. You don't talk out there at night, so I had drifted off, thinking about the beach at home. I could almost smell that rank odor of seaweed and dead fish washed up along the shore. It's funny, when it happened I was imagining myself floating out with the slow rock of swells lifting me up and dropping me down, and I swear the explosion seemed to come from a long way off. Truth is, Danny was only fifteen yards away, doing the sweep of the outside perimeter while I worked closer in. We'd only been there since the afternoon and hadn't found any mines. No one guessed the Cong had planted anything.

The force of the blast threw me to the ground, and it was a minute before I could lift my head. My ears were ringing and my eyes hurt. I called out Danny's name, but there was nothing. By then, the camp was juiced and moving. Three

47

guys came running, and in the dark I heard the rest of the platoon jamming clips into their M-16s. The medic was the first to get to him, but there was nothing anyone could do. Damn thing blew both legs completely off and threw a piece of shrapnel through his heart.

They relieved me for the night. They knew I was shaken. Shaken, hell, I was Jell-O. I couldn't even say my name when the medic first came over to check me out. I just sat there on the ground, clutching my rifle close to my chest. I was rocking. He put his hand on my shoulder and someone helped me up. With my arms draped over two other grunts, I made it back into the camp, lay down, and passed out.

The sun was just beginning to filter through the trees when I woke up. The lieutenant had doubled the patrol, but I don't think anyone except me slept that night. Danny was already wrapped up in a body bag, and I could hear the chopper coming in low across the valley. At first there was a low throb of engines, then steadily the sound grew into the thwok thwok thwok *of chopper blades slashing the heavy jungle air.*

Anyway, we're back, and the mission "sustained no other casualties." That's how we talk about it. Someone dies and we say we "sustained a casualty."

I've always wondered about the way we soften everything with the wrong words. We never say, "Dad's a drunk." We say, "Dad drinks." Do you see the subtle difference there? One is a problem that results in everything that makes your life and mine awful. The other is a statement that floats out there without judgment. Dad drinks and the family sustains casualties—you and me.

Before this, Jimmy, I've never had the sense that I could die. Now I do.

Frank

⅄

Last night, Dad "tied one on." Frank would call that a euphemism. *Euphemism.* I looked it up. It means to talk about something in terms that are less provocative than the thing itself.

We were at the dinner table and Dad was on his third bourbon and water. Mom was out at a Women's Club meeting. I think it's her way of staying sane, getting out of the house once a week. She never says much about what they do when they get together, but she's always in a good mood when she gets home. Usually, like last night, she puts dinner together and leaves it for us to warm up. Sometimes she instructs me carefully to order a pizza, but not to spend too much. I like those nights, because Dad lets me eat in front of the TV and I don't have to talk to him.

By the time Dad got home from work, I had the pork chops and vegetables ready to serve. I pulled the potatoes out of the oven just as he pulled up. While I set the table, he fixed a drink. By the time I got bread in the serving basket and tall glasses of water filled and set at each place, he was on his second. Now, while I ate my dinner and his remained untouched, he was working on number three. Ice cubes moved slowly around in the glass, shapes and shadows forming and unforming.

I read once that magazine ads will airbrush shapes of naked women into pictures of ice cubes in a glass of whiskey just to make it more appealing. Sitting there, chewing a gristly piece of pork chop and trying to see the next best thing to Jayne Mansfield reflected in the swirling ice, I wasn't paying attention when Dad asked for the potatoes.

"I'm talking to you," his voice came through the fog.

I was still stuck somewhere between subliminal advertising and how many times I should chew before swallowing.

"I'm talking to you," he said again.

There was gravel in his voice, a kind of slurry washed with muddy water.

"What?" I asked, looking up.

"Pass the goddamn potatoes."

When he starts to swear in the middle of simple requests, I know he's looped. I reached across the table and picked up the bowl, but it slipped and crashed down, rotating on the edge of its bottom like a slow-motion top.

"Can't even hold a goddamned bowl of potatoes. Jesus, sometimes I think you're as worthless as your brother. Pay attention to what you're doing, damn it."

I picked up the bowl again and handed it to him, standing in the same motion to leave the table.

"Where do you think you're going?" he asked.

"I'm not hungry," I said, and turned to go.

"You'll sit here and eat your dinner until I excuse you from the table," he said, grabbing the sleeve of my shirt as he spoke. I tried to pull away, but the cloth ripped and he dug his fingers into my arm.

"I already finished," I told him, knowing in advance that no amount of reason would have any effect on him now.

He spun me around and pushed me toward my chair. The chair had been pushed aside when he grabbed me and now I went crashing to the floor.

"Get up, goddamn it!" he shouted. "And don't talk back to me. Sit down or I'll knock you down."

Chapter 6

November 25, 1967
Da Nang

Jimmy,

I don't know how to say this without sounding melodramatic: I got hit. I took a bullet in the stomach and spent two weeks in bed, nurses running around, doctors checking this and that. For a while, they thought I was gone, but I'm tough stuff, you know that. Anyway, it's why I haven't written in a while.

I don't remember much about getting shot. We were on patrol, this time in the Mekong, sweeping the villages for Charlie. It was routine: move in, check out the huts, search the storage sheds, look for pits and mines. Everyone in the village was smiling. Kids ran around tugging on our sleeves. They wanted to see our dog tags and rifles. I carry a pocketful of candy with me to hand out when we come to one of these places, and I was Mister Happy. They loved me.

Then Charlie came out of the woods. Remember when we played war? How we looked at woods and imagined every tree as an enemy? That's exactly what this was. One minute we were playing good-guy American soldiers, and the next we were sitting ducks.

I was standing in the middle of the village with Tom, who just got back from R and R, and we were doing hand signs with a couple of women from the village. Kids were running around, chattering, dashing in and out of shadows. I remember the jungle was a lush shade of green, the sun like butter falling everywhere. Birds cried out from the trees, and overhead I heard the sound of jets.

Then it was silent. Just like that. One minute a burst of sound and movement, then nothing. Except, from behind every tree stepped a gook, gun blazing. Tom went down first, a look of complete surprise on his face. I looked at him and laughed, thinking, "Damn, don't play with me

53

like this." Then he was face-first in the dirt, blood spreading out from his head.

I couldn't move. Maybe if I'd moved, they wouldn't have gotten me. I don't know. Only one of us got out with nothing, and he can't talk, he's so freaked out. My buddies were falling all around me, and then I felt like someone lit me up. I bent over and hit the dirt. I hurt like I've never hurt before. They tell me it was only fifteen minutes before the choppers came and the Cong spread out, back into the jungle, as quiet and invisible as they'd been before they shot us full of holes, but it felt as if I were lying there for hours.

The hospital was actually a relief. They gave me morphine for the pain, which took care of it and then some. I don't know if it kept hurting or if I just got to like the shots, but every little while I found myself calling for the nurse. She'd come in and stick me, and next thing I knew, a kind of all-over good feeling of warmth swept through my body.

They stitched me up and let me lay around for a few days, then they sent me back to the front, whatever that is. We don't even know where the enemy is most of the time. That's why we cruise out through the jungle looking for him. Still, half the time he finds us before we find him.

For now I'm back at my post, not far from Da Nang. I'm feeling better and can get around pretty well. Until we're reassigned, we get up mornings when we want to, smoke pot, and listen to the radio. What the army sells as radio is mostly crap, but they do play some good tunes sometimes. When I hear the Doors blasting "Light My Fire," I want to get back home to Susan so bad it hurts.

Frank

⋀

As Frank's words sink in, I can feel the blood pounding in my ears. It's like the background sound of the world—that constant low hum—but it suddenly grows louder and becomes the only thing I can hear. I sit motionless for a long time in the big chair in the living room.

When Mom comes home, we sit together in the living room while the afternoon light fades into evening. Dad comes in around six and surveys the room.

"You both look like it's the end of the world," he says.

Mom hands him the letter Frank sent to them. Dad scans the letter, then looks out the window. Across the street, the neighbor kids are swinging a bat tied to a piece of rope, trying to knock a coconut from a low palm tree.

"It was only a matter of time," Dad says, turning his gaze back to the letter. "Idiot probably stood up in the middle of a gunfight. Made a target of himself."

"Jim . . . ," Mom begins. Her voice trails off and she starts to cry.

"Well, damn it. You know I'm right. Frank never did have any sense."

"Dad," I scream, "he's been *shot!*"

They both look at me.

"Don't raise your voice with me," Dad says, lifting his hand and curling his fingers into a fist.

Dad walks out to the kitchen. I can hear him pull the ice tray out of the freezer, pull the lever back to loosen the cubes, then drop three of them into a glass. I get up and head down the hall.

"Jimmy, are you okay?" Mom asks.

"Yeah. I'm fine, Mom," I reply over my shoulder, turning up the sarcasm in my voice until it goes off the scale.

⌃

Dad's not always a jerk. Occasionally, he brightens up and takes me to the beach for the day, or gathers Mom and me up for a drive out to Loxahatchee, where we watch herons and egrets swoop low above the saw grass. Those are the good days. Not something you can mark the calendar by—the way you might tick off the good moments against the bad—but good nonetheless.

Earlier this fall, when Hurricane Jesse was roaring toward the coast of Florida, we had one of those moments that almost makes me feel as if there's a chance for our family, a chance Dad will turn out to be a good guy after all, that Mom and Frank can stop living as if they have to fight with him or apologize for what he does. And maybe a chance that I can walk around the house without feeling like *I'm* the one who's a moving target.

When we got up that morning, I could tell Dad's head hurt, but he was smiling and seemed happy. Mom was out in the kitchen wrapping bologna sandwiches and putting them in a bag along with potato chips. On the floor, a bright red Coleman cooler rested with the lid propped open. Inside Mom had stacked bottles of Coke and some oranges and apples. Dad came in from the backyard and announced that we were heading over to the beach to watch the ocean as this new storm rolled in.

"We won't stay long," he said, "just enough to see it wild."

Mom was nervous, remembering how Betsy raged two years earlier, but I'm always on the lookout for waves. We loaded the cooler into the trunk of the car and pulled out of the driveway. Along the streets I noticed the wind had already begun to push trash into tight piles in the gutters. The palms in all the yards were waving. It was raining, but not hard, more like a heavy mist. We had our raincoats in the back seat and Mom had brought her umbrella. I remember thinking about Mary Poppins, wondering if she opened the umbrella if she'd fly away, or if it would just rip inside out like they do in the cartoons.

As we crossed the bridge and drove across to Singer Island, the intensity of the wind and rain picked up. The neighborhoods looked buttoned up, plywood on the windows and doors, practically no one in the yards. I imagined everything abandoned, evacuated, until just ahead I saw an old man on a ladder sawing away at the already dead branch of an Australian pine, cutting it off, I guess, so that it wouldn't break off in the storm and smash his roof. He looked bored or pissed off that he was out there in the rain. As he sawed, the branch caught in the wind, fell and skittered across the yard, finally coming to rest with the thick end in the street. Dad hit the brakes and swerved to miss it. The old man watched us, no change at all in his expression. I turned to look out of the rear window and watched him climb down from the ladder and with great effort pull the branch toward the side of the house.

Another block and we turned onto A1A. When the wind gusted, I could feel the car rock. Mom clenched her hand around the handgrip above the door.

"Jim," she said, "do you think this is a good idea?"

He didn't answer but kept on driving. The radio kept repeating warnings about how powerful Jesse was and how much havoc they expected her to wreak. I could see the tension in my mother's hand and follow it all the way up her arm to where the tendons in her neck tightened and stuck out. We drove past the Singer Island Pool and Racquet Club and turned into the parking lot of Delphina's restaurant.

Dad parked the car and turned to look at me.

"Ready to go, Junior?" he asked, more a directive than a question, but I was already halfway out the door.

The wind was blowing so hard I had to hold on with all I was worth just to keep the door from slamming shut. I was wearing a baseball hat, which I held with the other hand so it didn't fly across the highway. Mom sat in the front seat, hands clenched in her lap.

"You go ahead," she said. "I'll wait here."

I closed the door and followed Dad toward the beach. Waves the size of barns curled and crashed as far as I could see. Dad was out ahead and I hurried to catch up, but he was moving fast and didn't look back. After a couple of minutes, I slowed down and looked around. The waves were coming all the way up to the dunes. Already they'd chewed huge chunks of sand away, leaving sea grapes and clumps of grass hanging over the edge of newly formed drop-offs. It was hard to look straight out. Sand blew and the salt spray burned my eyes. I squinted and walked along the edge of the dune.

Just ahead, the waves had carved an indentation, a cave, out of the sand. Carefully, I climbed down the dune and scrambled around to the hollow. Roots entwined with shells and pieces of coral hung down from above. I crawled inside and sat, my back curved perfectly against the sand. Staring out at the raging Atlantic, I wondered: *If I start swimming, if I paddle my surfboard out and ride the currents, how long would it take to get to Frank?*

I forgot where I was until I noticed that my jeans were soaked and the waves were pushing farther up the beach. *This is a hurricane,* I thought. *I have to get out of here.* I reached up and grabbed a root to swing myself up, but the weight of my body was more than the sand could bear, and the ceiling of the cave collapsed. Next thing I knew, the water was swirling all around me. I grabbed for whatever I could hold, but there wasn't anything solid anywhere. The suck of current dragged me head-long toward the sea.

Then real panic set in. I was struggling against the undertow. I kicked with my legs and pulled for all I was worth with my arms. I was about to lose my breath when I felt something grip me and pull me from the tide. I opened my eyes and saw my father standing there, knee-deep in the frothy water, a look of fear I've never seen on his face before, holding onto me.

And then we were sitting in the car. I was soaked to the bone. Mom held out a sandwich. I tipped a bottle of Coke to my mouth. The carbonation ripped my throat, and I felt a kind of warmth coming back. Dad didn't say anything but sat entirely rigid in the driver's seat. Mom ran her fingers through my wet hair.

"Are you OK?" she kept asking.

"Yeah," I said, leaning toward the sandwich, mouth open. I'd never guessed near death would be so good for the appetite, but I was hungry.

Jesse hit hard that evening. Just as with Betsy two years before, we followed Mom's Plan. When we got home that afternoon, Dad covered up the windows with scraps of plywood and Mom filled the tub with water, which I always thought was kind of dumb. Who wants to drink out of their bathtub?

About nine o'clock, Dad was getting ready for bed. He had pulled on pajama bottoms and was standing in the living room, looking out into the dark rage of the storm. I came up behind him to say good night.

"You scared me today, Jimmy."

"I scared myself too," I said with a nervous laugh.

"It's bad enough Frank's gone off to Vietnam," he said. "I don't want to lose both of my boys."

He was quiet. The usual edge in his voice was missing. I stepped closer and touched him on the shoulder.

"Thanks for pulling me out, Dad."

"Yeah," he replied.

Throughout the night, the storm rose and howled. I lay in bed, trying hard to sleep. At some point, the wind drove under the plywood, ripping a piece loose. All night I could hear it, flapping and banging against the stucco wall.

Chapter 7

November 30, 1967
Near Pleiku

Jimmy,

It's late and I'm writing by flashlight. The nights here are so dark and long you almost forget you're in the middle of a war. Sometimes. Of course, there are nights when Charlie drops rockets on your position and you wake up like it's Judgment Day. On those nights there is one instant between sleeping and waking when you're still lost in a dream, but the dream starts to include explosions, and for that instant the explosions are peaceful, a part of that magical world that isn't sleep and isn't wakefulness, but something else. It's kind of like that moment when you're about to catch a wave: you can't really feel the momentum grab hold yet, but you know in a second you'll be up and carving.

The difference is that here, instead of catching a wave, you wake to a scramble, the whole camp up and running everywhere, pulling on shirts, grabbing rifles, disappearing into the trees. If I knew that I'd wake up from every dream to this nightmare for the rest of my life, I swear, Jimmy, I'd stand and wait for the rockets to find me.

A couple nights ago, we were dug in from a scare earlier in the day. Pretty secure, really. I had dropped off to the sound of a pack of monkeys playing somewhere in the dark. I listened as long as I could, thinking they're the only sane ones over here. I've watched them during the day. They shriek at each other, squeal like pigs, and then swing from branch to branch, chasing each other like a bunch of kids. We don't run across them often: they hide when people get too near. I don't know, but they say the VC shoot and eat them. Now, think about that for a minute—someone hunts you down to kill you, and rather than turning around and trying to hunt them down, you simply disappear, you hide. Somehow it seems to me that makes a lot more sense than what we do. At least when the Cong are full, they stop shooting monkeys, and the monkeys are safe for a while. Not us. It doesn't have a damn thing to do with being hungry—we shoot each other until we run out of bullets or bodies.

I woke up in the middle of the night and had to pee. The monkeys were still shrieking and scampering around out there, even though by now they had quieted down a little. I got up and walked over to a tree just outside the encampment. While I was standing there taking care of business, the monkeys suddenly shut up. I didn't think much of it at first, but within seconds the first rocket plowed into the camp. Somebody screamed and everyone was up and crashing through the jungle, looking for anywhere a rocket might not fall. It's a crapshoot. You could stay right in camp and never get hit. Or you could dash a hundred yards into the smothering trees and find yourself at ground zero.

The lieutenant got on the radio and called in the fighters. It always amazes me how fast those guys can get to wherever we are. Within five minutes I could hear the air start to hum, and then the bombs started banging down on Charlie's head as the jets zipped over. It was over in less than *fifteen minutes, start to finish. I sat there under that tree for the rest of the night, smack dab in the middle of my own piss. At dawn, soaking wet and cold, I shook the numbness off and stumbled back into camp. Most everyone else was already there, a few rubbing their eyes like they were waking up at the Holiday Inn.*

When I get back, I'm going to surf until my skin shrivels up. I'll sit there all day waiting, and I'm not sure anymore it's going to be so much about the wave itself. I think I'll catch everything I can just to prove that I can come out of that moment of possibility into the sweet slide on the face of the ocean rather than into the earsplitting whistle of a rocket.

Frank

⋀

After dinner tonight, I wash the dishes and clean my room. When I come back out to the living room, Mom has set out the Monopoly game, hopeful, I think, that we might sit down like a real family, play a game and laugh and talk, maybe clear the air from all the funk Dad's been spewing since Frank got shot.

She's cleared the coffee table and unfolded the board, carefully lining the edges up with the edges of the table.

Mugs of hot chocolate with big globs of marshmallow melting across the surface are steaming on a TV tray beside the couch. Dad is sitting in his big brown chair with a drink in his hand, moving the glass in slow circles, watching the ice swirl around.

I claim the game piece that looks like an old shoe. It's my favorite. Call me superstitious, but I've always believed that if you take a humble piece—the worn-out shoe, the iron—fate will smile on you as you play, rewarding humility with hotels on Boardwalk and Park Place. Dad picks out the racecar and Mom takes the wheelbarrow.

We start to play. I roll the dice and move. Dad rolls and moves. Mom sits dreamily, looking down the hall.

"Would you *move?*" Dad says.

Even *games* in this family turn into little wars. I could feel the tension rising and thought about Frank, nine thousand miles away. Dad swirled his drink, took a swallow, and glared at Mom.

She turns her head slowly until her eyes meet his.

"It's my turn?" she asks.

⅄

Once, in the summer before we moved to Florida, when vacation meant long days playing in the field and the woods behind our house, I came down with a flu that wouldn't let me out of bed or off the couch for at least a week. Each night when Dad got home from work, after he had read the paper, we would play Monopoly. One evening, we were well into the game; Dad was about to put hotels on some hot property and put me out of business. Frank came in the door—he'd been out riding his bike with Mike Stevens from next door—threw his baseball glove on the couch, pulled off his sneakers, and walked out to the kitchen without saying a word to either my dad or me. He had reached into the refrigerator for the Tupperware pitcher of water Mom kept cold in there. Dad put down the dice, stood up, stormed into the kitchen, swiped the bottle from Frank's hand, and stared hard at him as it fell to the floor.

"Do you think this place is a dump?" Dad screamed. "Who's going to pick up your crap? Your mother? Me? Now get in there and pick that stuff up."

I know this doesn't make sense, but sometimes I think Dad has tried since Frank was little to impose an order on Frank's life that he has been unable to find in his own. At any rate, his reaction to my brother tossing his glove and sneakers around was way out of proportion to the act itself. Of course, I was ten at the time and only wanted to get out of the way.

Frank stood there like a statue. His mouth was partly open, his eyes opened wide and shiny as marbles. Dad didn't flinch, and finally Frank took one step toward the living room. That's when he smacked Frank.

"Are you going to clean your mess up, or am I going to have to smack you again?"

I could see a welt already coming up on Frank's cheek where Dad had hit him. He didn't say anything. He didn't cry. But you could see the hatred in his eyes.

Finally, he slouched and the tension drained out of him.

"I'll clean it up," he said. "But don't you ever hit me again."

He pulled a towel from the rack on the kitchen wall and started wiping up the water. Dad sat back down and rolled his dice, as if nothing out of the ordinary had happened. I kept looking out at Frank, who snuck a glance at me occasionally.

⁓

Now, Dad plunks his glass on the table and I snap out of the memory. I don't feel like playing anymore, but I roll the dice and wind up in jail on my third move. It's all downhill from there. Dad buys a whole row of stuff—Marvin Gardens, Indiana—and Mom does her usual job of acting like she just can't figure it out, letting him walk all over her. I lose my last ten bucks and go to bed.

Chapter 8

January 1, 1968
Da Nang

Jimmy,

Just before Christmas, I got leave and went to Saigon. It was amazing. I mean, there's Da Nang, where I came in, but it's just not that big and it's full of Americans. Saigon is really another world. What's weird is that I sort of forgot to think the Vietnamese might actually be civilized. A few weeks in the bush and you start to see them all as farmers just three steps out of the Stone Age. They're nice enough, and smart, when you can talk to them, but the villages are isolated and primitive.

In the city, everything moves. Markets line the streets; there are restaurants and street vendors everywhere—the smells of cooking oil and hot garlic fill the air. Little kids run around like there's nothing wrong with their country. For them this is normal. . . . All they've ever known is war. But they do know something's wrong. They stop us and ask us questions. They beg for money. They offer to sell us drugs and girls. All the while, when I look into their eyes, I can see the little kids they want to be staring out, scared as hell.

It's a busy city. Buildings slump together, jamming every square inch. Signs in Vietnamese and French and English bristle from the storefronts, offering everything from rope sandals to Paris fashions. The streets are wall-to-wall bicycles, people with baskets balanced across their shoulders on a stick, little French cars zooming in and out of traffic like a stock-car race. I only had three days, but I found a hotel room for next to nothing and went out exploring.

Ever since I got shot, the pain won't let go. For a while, the docs gave me morphine, then later some pills. I guess they thought it was enough and quit giving me anything a few weeks back. But it

71

kept hurting; even pot didn't take my mind off the pain. I'm telling you this because I tried something in Saigon I swore I'd never do. A boy about your age stopped me on the street and asked me in good English if I wanted to buy some smack. Remember how we talked back home about that stuff? That the only guys who'd touch it were junkies? Well, the pain was back like someone twisting broken glass inside me, and I bought a little bag from him. Just like the morphine (which is really what heroin is), it killed the pain.

All your life you hear about how you can get addicted to this stuff, how it can kill you. And then you find yourself with a lot of pain in the middle of a war that doesn't make any sense at all, and you try it.

And you know what? I've never felt so good. It's incredible. I don't know what we were talking about back then. What's wrong with feeling good?

Frank

⋏

Smack. Junk. Horse. It's hard for me to picture Frank, on leave in Saigon, holed up in some cheap hotel, drinking whiskey and shooting heroin. Not because I can't conjure up the *image*—it *hurts* to think he's doing something so stupid. I mean, all the kids here talk about drugs, but it's pot and acid, stuff that's supposed to open your mind up, not drag it down. Just before he left, Frank told me if he didn't join the army, he was going to Haight-Ashbury in San Francisco. It's where the kids are going who are tired of the way things are in America. I don't know exactly what they're complaining about, but California sounds pretty cool. Mostly it's about hanging out and listening to music. And they protest the war. That much I understand.

But I don't understand the drugs. I've never wanted to feel any different from the way I do. I like to know where I am and how long it's going to take me to say my name if anyone asks. The idea of fireworks going off inside my head scares me.

Still, when Frank first smoked pot, I didn't know what to think. On the one hand, I didn't think it was a good idea, but my parents hated everything about drugs and the hippies, and that was enough to make me curious; if Dad hated it so much, there was bound to be something interesting going on. Which is probably why Frank got started in the first place. By then, he was so sick of being in the grip of Dad's failures that he'd do just about anything to break out. But even the hippies didn't trust narcotics.

I understand why Frank said yes to the boy with the heroin: he hurt. But I think the hurt is more than just the pain from getting shot. Just being there is getting to him, and I guess he doesn't know how to deal with it. In some of his earlier letters he comes right out and says it: how hard it is to shoot at people he can't think of as enemies, how hard it is to be in a war he doesn't believe in.

He's seen little kids blown away, mothers holding babies gunned down while they ran for cover, whole villages torched with napalm. I see it on the news; he sees it up close and personal. Being there, where you can smell the fire and the blood. . . . Maybe that's enough to make anyone go crazy.

⁁

Frank always seemed to hurt when someone else was hurting. From the time we were little, he picked up dogs and brought them home because they looked lonely. He rescued lizards when our cat Blondie had them dead to rights, pinned with the claws of one paw and swatting them with the other. As we got older, he did things that made the others kids his age look at him funny. He helped old ladies across the street. He carried books for the girls at school. Well, the pretty ones anyway.

Last year, before he enlisted, we were surfing by the *Amaryllis* when one of the guys about a hundred feet away was suddenly dragged from his board, screaming at the top of his lungs. He surfaced a couple of times and went back under before anyone realized what was happening. Who knows why, but even though sharks almost never come in that close to shore, one had been attracted to the kicking legs flashing from the side of the board. Maybe it thought the board was some big fish and would make a good dinner, but whatever it was, in two seconds surfing out there changed forever.

What was amazing to me, though, was how everyone else took off for shore, yelling in utter terror, while Frank paddled to where the guy was still flailing at the water, grabbed him by the arm, and dragged him slowly toward the beach. He didn't know whether the shark was finished. He told me later he didn't even think about it. He simply went in the direction he was needed.

We were sitting in the den when Dad came home that night. Apparently, Mom had already told him the story, because he was ripe and ready to burst when he came through the door.

"Don't you realize you could have been killed?" he shouted, taking two steps toward Frank.

He stopped and just stood there. Then something happened I don't think I've ever seen my father do when he was sober. He walked the rest of the distance to Frank and hugged him. Frank said later he didn't know what to do, what to feel. It was the first time he remembered Dad ever giving him a hug.

Two weeks later, Frank enlisted. It was late June,

just four weeks after he'd graduated. I'd started classes already and envied my brother for staying home and going surfing whenever he wanted to. I came home that afternoon—Friday—and Frank was sitting in the big papasan chair in the den. He had pamphlets and sheets of paper scattered all around him.

"Hey, Joon," he said, motioning me to come over to where he was, "you should have seen the waves today. Five, six feet, and sets rolling in one after the other." He'd been out by the ship again, the first time since the shark attack, and he was psyched.

Little by little the surfers had been moving back toward the grounded freighter, as if the jinx had a time limit. I hadn't wanted to go back; I didn't like thinking of my feet as shark food. The doctors had managed to sew the guy's foot back on, and he was up and hobbling around now on crutches, but he'd never walk normally again.

I watched Frank as he thumbed through a pamphlet.

"What's that?" I asked him.

"Army stuff," he said, not looking up. "I went to the recruiting office today and talked to some guy."

I looked at him sitting there, legs sprawled over the edge of the cushion, head laid back at an angle.

"Are you nuts?" I asked.

Pictures from the news flashed through my head: soldiers trudging waist-deep through swampy fields, ducking when the jets came in low and firebombed a village;

helicopters smacking at the air while medics loaded body bags into gaping doors.

"You can't sign up," I said. "They wouldn't take you."

I was thinking about his pot smoking, how he hated the army and the war, how he wanted to go to Haight-Ashbury.

He looked up then and smiled. It was a freaky smile, full of peace and decision.

"I already did," he said.

Chapter 9

April 10, 1968
Da Nang

Jimmy,

  I keep thinking about the old war movies we used to watch, where all the soldiers were in it together, fighting for democracy and America. What's weird is that no one seems to believe in this war at all. Oh, a few guys do, officers and some gung-ho warriors, but mostly everyone is baffled. Why are we here in the first place? What the hell does Vietnam have to do with the safety of American women and children?

And if we're going to be here, then why don't they let us really fight? We do these missions, stomping two weeks through the jungle, rounding up villagers like criminals when all they're trying to do is grow food and raise their kids, and then we come out and sit around the base, smoking pot, patching up the wounded, resting, and getting nervous, because as soon as we get comfortable, we get to go out and do it all over again. What's the point?

We almost never actually see Charlie. He's too damned smart, hiding in the trees like a monkey, living off the jungle until we crash into his area, and then all hell breaks loose. Half the time, we can't even see where he's coming from. We never hear him, never know when he'll pop up out of a rice paddy spraying bullets like some kind of nightmare. But he always knows where we are. He hears us crashing like a bunch of lumberjacks through the trees. Or he smells us. Can you believe that? He can smell the milk and meat we toss down every meal sweating out of our skin like a homing signal. It reminds me of bloodhounds tracking Nevada Smith through the swamp. The only thing chasing him, though, was a bunch of prison guards with IQs somewhere down around their knees. That, and his conscience. He wanted to kill—he had a reason. Here, none of us really know what we're fighting for.

I had a dream last night. We were out on Singer and the waves were huge. You and I sat side by side in the rising and sinking swells, waiting for the next big set. The shadow of the Amaryllis spread out over the water like night. It got darker and darker, and pretty soon we couldn't see the shore. I kept telling you it was all right, but you seemed to be less scared than I was. Then, all of a sudden, a swell swept you up and away and I was there by myself. I called you, but you didn't answer. I thought if I could get over to the ship, I could inch my way along the hull until I got back to the beach but, no matter how hard I paddled, I couldn't find it. After a while, I realized I'd been washed out to sea. There were stars and a half moon rising. Even though it was pitch dark, I could see moonlight glittering on the waves, but there was nothing anywhere, just water. Then, as suddenly as you'd disappeared, you showed up again. You were laughing, smiling. You didn't say anything, but you waved me toward you and we started paddling together toward whatever you seemed to know that I didn't. It started getting lighter and I could hear kids playing by the shore. I don't know what it all meant, but as soon as you turned up again, I knew I'd be OK.

I've been dreaming a lot lately. Some pretty awful stuff, actually. Sometimes it's personal; mostly it's the war. I think the war has a way of getting inside our heads, some of us worse than others. Sometimes I'm afraid I'll carry it forever. The smack helps. There's a guy in my unit who has a steady supply. I hurt, Jimmy. I hurt and I hurt and I hurt. And I visit the guy with the supply. And I shoot it up. And then I don't hurt. For a while I don't hurt.

Frank

∧

April 25, 1968
Mekong Delta

Dear Jimmy,

I sometimes think if I just stood still I'd sink into the jungle here and become a part of it like everything else. And sometimes when the smack is running in my blood, I think I already have. I get up in the morning soaked from night sweats, shaking, put on damp clothes, and fire up a little junk to get ready for a new day's sweat.

Everything here is wet. Rice paddies, saw grass, jungle, coastal marshes . . . everything. And hot. If it's not raining, then I drip from the inside out; if it's raining, I drip from the outside in. Either way, there's never any letup. By noon almost every day, it starts. Black clouds like flowers open up and drop great sheets of water down. We cover up with ponchos, but it doesn't make any difference. Except, I guess, to keep our weapons dry. Or reasonably dry.

Man, that's the toughest part. The lieutenant checks our weapons constantly. If they're wet or dirty, we have to tear them down and clean them. But I've got to tell you, there's no amount of oil that can keep them working.

Last week, out on patrol, we ran into a VC unit. They were holed up outside a village we had thought was friendly. It's so hard to tell over here because we can't talk to any of the natives, and there are plenty of stories about friendlies turning up with bombs or poisoned food. Anyway, we were moving, single file, along a footpath near the river. Out on the water we could hear the growl of a patrol boat, and through the trees we could see some locals pushing long, low boats loaded with bananas along the shore. A bunch of monkeys were making a racket in the trees down by the river.

Out of the blue, I felt the hot trail of a bullet whiz by my face, and I dropped. The whole patrol dropped except the point man. I could see him through a break in the palmetto fronds, standing as if he was frozen. Following his eyes off into the trees, I could see a VC hunched in the scrub. From somewhere deep in the jungle, one of those damned lizards screamed, Fuck you. *Like it was slow motion, I watched our guy, Simmons, lifting his gun, bringing it up to his shoulder, sighting along the barrel, squeezing the trigger. Nothing happened. He looked down, his face a sudden mask of surprise, and started to reach for the clip, I guess to see if it was jammed. But you only get one chance out here; before he could get his hand up to the stock of the rifle, the VC opened up and ripped his face apart. I've never seen anything so awful. Simmons stood there for a split second—it seemed as if he was still looking at his gun—and then he crumpled to the ground.*

The VC must not have wanted a fight right then. We lay low for a few minutes, trying to get a read on their position, but when one of our guys crawled forward to scout them, all he found was a cleared place in the jungle where they'd been eating lunch. By the time we got to Simmons, ants had already swarmed his face; they were almost swimming in the blood. When the lieutenant checked his weapon, he found mud in the firing mechanism, not much, but enough to keep the round from entering the chamber. Enough to kill him.

It was a bad week out there. Since we were near Saigon, we all got two days leave. By the time I got there, I was shaking. I keep thinking I'll forget the heroin, but my body remembers. I wasn't in town more than fifteen minutes before I scored. Good China White. The next two days were a dream. The other guys went out and partied, hitting the bars, dancing, but me . . . well, I hung in my room, lost in a daze, my own little monkey clawing at my back.

When I'm in it, Jimmy, when the buzz is running through my body, it's like the rest of the world evaporates. It feels good. I forget the jungle and the gooks, the rain and the sound of automatic weapons splitting the air around me. I forget about Tom. I forget about everything except Florida.

Imagine that, Florida as the dream that keeps me going. God, I hated that place, mostly, I guess, because of Dad, but also because it's so slow and old. I used to think I'd get out of high school and immediately turn sixty, get a place in a retirement village, start playing shuffleboard during the day and bridge at night—you know, just skip everything in between. Now I almost wish I could. Sometimes when I'm nodding, a load of smack coursing through my brain, I think perhaps I could just do thirty years like this, then stop and wind up retired and happy. No memory of Nam, no bullshit job back home, no pain.

Of course, there's the other side. When I'm out with my platoon, and it's been a few days, a week, whatever, my body remembers what I'm trying to forget—how good the junk makes me feel—and I start to jones. I shake and sweat, my head feels like a cheap balloon, and I think if something doesn't happen soon I'm going to explode. And then we walk into some stupid ambush or a bunch of gooks just having lunch, and I'm right back in it—war in all its glory. Another week and the shakes aren't so bad, but by then I'm screaming inside, with the blood and the dying running around like horrible circus clowns, and all I can think about is getting back to Saigon or finding the guy I know on base who sells, so I can lose myself all over again in the haze.

Jimmy, I want out. Out of Nam, out of this

God-awful need, out of the pain. What happened
to waxing a surfboard and paddling into a rising
sun, waiting for the perfect set, for that wave that
catches your tail and pushes you like some ancient
god toward shore?

I miss it, Jimmy. I miss it all.

Frank

All winter and spring, I've been walking to the beach
with Terry, my best friend, who lives in Lake Park. It's a
hike, but it beats talking Dad into a ride, and besides,
this way Terry and I get to stop at Dunkin' Donuts and
drink coffee, something Mom still tells me I'm too
young for.

This morning, everything is still. The sky is dark with
heavy clouds like dirty wads of cotton. It's early for the
summer rains, but a storm ripped up the coast last night,
reminding us that hurricane season is only a couple
months away.

It's only a couple miles from my house to Terry's, but
some days it feels like a hundred. I manage to get out of
the house without Dad seeing me. He always tries to get
me into shorts and sneakers, but I feel stupid like that.
Tourists wear shorts in Florida, not residents. I've got
new jeans on today. Some kids buy them and wash them

twenty times with bleach to get that faded, worn look, but I've got a better idea.

"Hey man," Terry says when we meet at his house and head toward the causeway. "What are you looking so busted up about?"

I kick a pop can that's lying in the gutter. It bounces for a few feet, then splashes into a shallow puddle.

"Nothing. I'm fine," I say.

"If you looked any lower, I'd be scraping you off the sidewalk. . . ." His words drifted off. "Look at that!" he exclaims, waving his hand toward Federal Highway.

A funeral procession is moving slowly south, a big black hearse out front and a line of limousines following. Two motorcycle cops head up the line of vehicles.

"I wonder who died."

"Probably some big shot from Palm Beach," I venture.

"Yeah, maybe," he says. "Come on, what's going on with you?"

"Nothing, man, I'm good."

By now the sun is beginning to erase the clouds. It's getting hot. And it's so humid it feels like you could wring water from the air. By the time we get across the bridge, it's searing hot, especially for May, and my feet are burning from the blacktop. I've learned from living here two years to find the lightest-colored anything to walk on, so I hop up on the sidewalk where there is sidewalk, and cool my feet in grass whenever we pass someone's yard. There are guys like Terry who walk the length of A1A barefoot every day and never wince, but I don't think I'll ever grow the calluses he's got.

Finally, we get to the beach.

"Come on," he hollers. "Race you."

We cross A1A at a dead run to beat the traffic and hit the sand full speed, careening toward the water like a couple of drunken monkeys.

"Hallelujah!" he shouts at the top of his lungs, and dashes the last few feet.

I'm right behind him, kicking up sand with every step, forgetting the heat. I hit the water and thrash my way out to where Terry is splashing. I don't know how long we swim down and back along the beach, going out to where the waves turn into swells the size of hills, carrying us up, then sliding us down. After a while, I roll over on my back and lay there floating, looking up at the sky, which by now has almost completely cleared, the sun like a furnace crouched directly overhead.

I search the water for Terry but don't see him anywhere, and then, maybe a hundred yards away, I find him settled into a slow Australian crawl, heading for the *Amaryllis*. I climb out of the water and stumble up the dune, my new jeans sticking to my legs like glue. The way I figure it, they'll come out looking worn, and they'll shrink to fit me perfectly if I let them dry while I'm wearing them.

I lay back in the sand and close my eyes. School is almost over for another year. Next year I'll be a junior. The next a senior. Progression.

Last time I was here after a storm, Frank was too. I don't talk too much about him with Terry. They didn't know each other well, and I don't really know what to say. How do you tell your best friend that your brother's doing smack? "Hey, Terry, Frank's got a new habit. . . ."

The sun lulls me like I'm drifting on a boat, and I imagine looking up at sails a hundred feet in the air, billowing with wind, driving the boat toward Africa. And then I'm standing on the rail, my hand cupped over my eyes to block the sun, and I'm staring hard at the horizon, where a tiny black dot is bobbing in and out of sight. I know somehow it's Frank, floating on a raft he's built from bamboo and rope, but the faster I go, the farther away he seems to drift. I don't know who's piloting the sailboat, but I have faith they will guide the boat in the right direction, so I continue to watch over the railing.

The day goes on, and the sun begins to drop. I can see Frank's arms waving in the distance like a pair of semaphore flags, but we don't seem to be any closer. All night, the boat slices through the sea, and I stand there motionless.

I realize now there's nothing I can do to reach Frank, and a sense of horror creeps up inside my stomach. I want to yell, to scream at anything at all, but there's nothing anywhere except water and darkness and the quiet swoosh of water lapping up against the boat. I sit down on the planking that forms the deck and try to follow the seams from where I sit to the bow and then back toward the stern. They slip away in both directions into nothingness; suddenly the boat is so immense I can't even walk from one side to the other.

"Frank, you bastard!" I yell, crying now and banging my hands against the deck.

⋏

I wake up to the sound of a radio. Terry is over me with a girl I recognize from school. She's got a transistor radio and the Beatles are on, singing "Strawberry Fields Forever." I rub my eyes, disoriented and startled to find myself on dry land, burnt to a crisp from the sun.

"Hey, man," Terry says, waving a hand at the girl, "do you know Sally?"

Chapter 10

Jimmy,

You should be here for the rain. I mean, if Nam was a day in the park before, it's got to be heaven now. Two weeks and practically no break in the downpour. We wake up in rain, brush our teeth in rain, march in rain, clean our weapons in rain, breathe, sleep, dream, and fight in rain.

We just got back from a mission in the Mekong. At times, I was walking in mud up past my ankles. Every so often, one of the guys would lose a boot and have to dig around in the muck until he found it, then rinse it in a muddy pool and put it back on. You get to the point where you can't imagine anything dry. And then you get to the point where you think you're drowning with every breath. And then you get to the point where none of it matters. I'm kind of like that all the time these days.

Last week, a guy from another unit bought it in the middle of a field. It was a quiet morning, not a sign of Charlie, and we were patrolling the perimeter of an area we supposedly secured a month ago. I had stopped for a drink of water and was leaning against a tree just inside the edge of the jungle. It was weird because the rain had stopped and the sun was hard as steel the way it crashed down in the clearing. That's the thing over here: you think we've got humidity in Florida, forget it. Here, the sun comes out and all the mud and standing water start climbing at dawn until by nine in the morning you feel like you're walking through a sponge.

Anyway, this guy was walking across the field toward me, waving, when all of a sudden a rocket dropped and exploded right next to him. Then the air erupted with the stutter of rifles and auto-

matic weapons and I sprawled out on the ground digging to get my gun ready. Our lieutenant hollered, "Nobody move," and we lay there, pinned by a blind attack. After a while the gunfire slowed down and I could hear this guy—the one who was crossing the field—not ten yards from me. He'd been thrown by the blast. I could hear him groaning and begging for help. I managed to inch up to where I could see him: he was leaning against a little rise in the ground—an anthill or something—completely covered in blood.

The lieutenant ordered us to hold our positions, and we did. For what seemed like hours we lay right where we were, while this guy moaned and cried. After that first round of fire, there was nothing. I couldn't tell if Charlie was still out there or not. It was so still I could hear a guy pinned behind me breathing. The sun beat down and the grass waved in a heavy breeze, but no one moved. Little by little, the steady hum of insects started up again, and then the sky darkened and the rain began to fall.

Pretty soon, we got word to circle back and try to find the spot where the attack came from. As I raised myself up and stood, I stopped and stared for a long time at the guy who had been crossing the field. He'd quit making any sound at all, and I knew he was dead. I could see he'd lost a leg and part of one arm, and I thought again of that kid by the Amaryllis. If I'd gone out there to get this guy, would he be okay? What is happening to me? A living, breathing boy my own age walks across a field with a smile on his face and buys the big one. And what do I do? I hide in the tall grass and trees, waiting for the shooting to stop, listening to him beg me to come and get him. Jimmy, I listened to him die. And the whole time I was shaking from the inside out because I needed a fix.

We moved out and found where the enemy had lain in wait for us: the hollowed-out places in the grass where they crouched, now filled with spent ammo cartridges. All day, we worked our way through villages and fields where the villagers were working the soggy earth, and all day the rain continued. By nightfall we were camped outside a village where a woman had waved at us and then carried, with the help of three small children, baskets of bread and food and bottles of wine for us. I didn't understand anything she was saying, but I had to turn away from the guys in my unit so they wouldn't see me cry.

I never thought much about life one way or another. You just take it for granted, and then *one day you're stuck in the middle of a pointless war, and death becomes a thing you listen to like insects, or a breeze riffling the leaves of trees. And still, as common as it becomes, as often as it whisks by you in the night while you're sleeping or brushes against you during the day while you're on patrol, you come to loathe it. As you get used to it, you hate it and fear it. And when you fear it, you turn away from life, too, because you can't have one without the other. Maybe that's not exactly right. You don't turn away from life, but you start to fear it as much as you do death. Problem is, here there's so much of one and not enough of the other, so everything gets mixed up.*

Smack is another way of turning away. I can't stand it anymore, Jimmy. I'm scared. I can't even walk without a good buzz. I shoot up when I get up in the morning. I shoot up on patrol. I shoot up so I can sleep. Between the war and the smack, I don't think there's much left of me.

Frank

⅄

After Terry and Sally came up to where I was sleeping on the beach, we sat for a long time and talked, drinking cold Cokes that Sally had brought with her from the

7-Eleven across A1A. More accurately, they talked and I listened. And I watched Sally: long, blond hair down the middle of her back, sun-browned skin. And the way the sun flickered in her eyes made me crazy. I tried, but couldn't even open my mouth to speak.

I don't know why I have so much trouble talking around girls, but it never fails. Inside, I'm full of the right things to say, but when I open my mouth, something stupid comes out. So I've learned to button up. Of course, the problem with that is that other boys always sweet talk the girls, and I wind up walking down the beach alone.

Sure enough, that's what was happening today too. Terry talked. Sally talked. She was full of energy and came back at Terry after everything he said. They were going on about the war, and Sally started telling us about her brother, who was three years older and had gone to the university in Tallahassee. She had a way of talking that seemed wise and sure. She would pause in the middle of a sentence and look straight into my eyes, giving what she was saying a chance to sink in.

"Protests," she said, "every day, almost. . . . John says the students show up by the thousands . . . waving signs and singing Joan Baez songs."

"Yeah, the hippies are taking over America," Terry said with mock alarm.

Sally laughed, and I got up and headed for the water.

I was almost at the tide line, seaweed scattered in long, sweeping curves where the water pushed and then retreated, when I sensed Sally right behind me, running.

"Come on," she yelled when she caught up with me, then grabbed my hand and dragged me toward the water.

I started running too, and we charged and splashed until the water came up higher than our knees. I plunged in and dove underwater as far out as I could. My heart was doing double time.

When I came up, she was not more than five feet away, treading water and looking at me funny, not saying anything.

"What?" I said, surprised that she had kept up with me; I'm a good swimmer.

"What happened to you back there?" she asked. "I was talking about John, and you just got up and left. I think that's pretty rude."

I knew she wasn't really mad, because she smiled while she talked. And her eyes were doing that sundance thing. So then I started talking. I started and I couldn't stop. I told her about Frank. I told her about my father and how Frank had enlisted to get away from him, how everything had gone wrong for Frank over there, that he couldn't stand the pain and the death, and I was worried about him. I told her about the heroin.

"Wow," she said, hushed by this last part. "How can he be doing that and still be fighting?"

"I think a lot of the guys are doing it. Like escaping from how awful everything is over there."

"Yeah, I guess," she said, "but what if he gets shot again? I mean, doesn't being high affect your reactions and everything?"

"That's what I've been worried about," I said.

⌒

Why it is I can't tell Terry about what's going on with my brother and then I can turn around and tell a girl I've almost never talked to my deepest secrets, I don't know. I suppose it's connected to the open-my-mouth-and-say-something-stupid syndrome that makes me usually keep my mouth shut. Maybe girls scare me because once I start talking I can't stop. Or maybe I just knew somehow that Sally would understand. Whatever it is, there I was, floating up and down on the swells, telling Sally my whole life story. And she didn't seem to get bored or impatient; she just listened and smiled.

I could see Terry back on the beach, sipping his Coke and reading a book. Every so often, I'd catch him looking at us and he'd wave. The horizon rose and sank with the ocean swells, and we rose and sank, gently, finally turning back toward shore, swimming slowly now, letting the waves carry us.

For the rest of the day, we walked along the water's edge or crossed A1A to get more Cokes or climbed up the railing at the corner of the pier and walked out to the end, where a few old men stood fishing.

We were staring at the horizon, straining to make out what kind of boats were bobbing there like giant, distant versions of the red-and-white bobbers the old men had tied to their fishing lines. She took my hand. Not the way she did earlier when she grabbed me to pull me into the sea, but different—soft, a little scared. I turned to look at her. She was still smiling; it seemed there was something in her that was always smiling.

"You're not alone," she said.

Terry was waiting where we had thrown our towels out, an indentation in the dune carved out by wind and water. The three of us walked across the road when Sally's mom pulled up to get her.

"I'll be here next Saturday at noon," Sally said to me as she got into the car.

Terry and I waved as they drove off.

"So, dude, stealing my girlfriend, eh?" Terry said.

"Like it was hard to win her away from you," I teased.

"So, what happened? What did you talk about?"

"None of your business."

"Oh, so now it's none of my business?" he said, poking me in the ribs.

"Just leave it alone."

By the time we got to Federal, weekend workers were getting off work and heading home. Usually we hitch-hiked from here, but today I wanted to walk.

"Listen, man," I told Terry finally, after he'd asked me for the millionth time, "I don't know if she likes me or if she'll forget before she gets home. Besides, like I said, it's none of your business."

All of this was new to me. Something about the way Sally grabbed my hand and tore off with me into the water twisted me up in knots I wasn't sure I could untie. Something too about the way she watched me and, when she spoke, said things that cut right to the heart of whatever I was feeling.

Terry and I always talked about girls. I'd never had any reason to clam up, but now I couldn't say a thing because my stomach and my heart were both doing back flips and I couldn't get anything settled down long enough to figure out what was happening.

We walked along Federal, passing the long rows of one-story buildings with plate-glass windows like gaping mouths open to the street. The rain and wind from the storm last night had stirred up everything. Palm trees looked like fat, gray fingers bent toward the ground, some of them stripped bare of fronds. The gutters along the sidewalk were filled with junk of every kind. We made a game for a while of trying to find certain things. Bottles, paper clips, cigarettes . . . all the usual stuff was there, but the fun was trying to find things that you didn't usually find. Money, shoes, model airplanes, kids' toys, condoms . . . we found it all.

"You know," I said, "I don't get it."

"What?"

"How it is we go hang out at the beach and drink Cokes, while Frank is over there dodging bullets."

"So, Sally's speech about the protests got to you?"

"No, it's not that."

"Well, what then?" he asked.

"I don't know. I can't explain it."

Through the front windows of some of the buildings, we could see men and women hurrying around, probably trying to make sure nothing blew away in the storm. Terry wanted to stop at Dunkin' Donuts, but I wasn't in the mood. The waitress we always flirt with was on duty, but the thought of drinking coffee and making stupid jokes with her made me feel uncomfortable.

Now Terry is leaning against his father's car in their driveway.

"So, you're not going to tell me anything, are you?"

"Man, just leave it alone."

"Did you kiss her?"

"I told you, it's none of your business."

"What's up with you? Is it Frank?"

"I've got to get home."

He's still leaning on the car, rubbing a spot on the hood with the tail of his T-shirt.

"Yeah," I say. "It's Frank."

"You want to talk about it?"

"No."

⌢

The sun is still high above the line of trees out west that mark the beginning of the Everglades. I head west to 441 instead of back to Federal. As I walk, my mind wanders away from Frank and Vietnam. Just walking alone along the road is good. Out here, the woods are still thick. The few scattered houses seem carved out of wilderness. I like to walk along the road with nothing else moving for miles.

My jeans are tight and stiff against my legs. I look at them from every angle I can, trying to see if they've faded at all. Of course, one trip into the sea might not be enough to do the work of Clorox, but I have other weekends. I already know I'm going back next weekend. Sally made sure of that.

Occasionally a car comes along, the hot wind it drags

behind it still tugging at me for a second after it's rushed by. One car stops and some middle-aged guy wearing a John Deere ball cap offers me a ride. I tell him no. It's one of those lessons my dad taught me that I actually listen to. Hitchhiking on Federal is one thing, but taking a ride with some pervert on a back road in the middle of nowhere is a different thing altogether. I don't know how long it takes me to get from Lake Park to North Palm, but by the time I turn to walk up through Palm Beach Gardens, the air is starting to cool and the pavement isn't so hot against my feet.

Cooler or not, my jeans are damp and heavy, this time with sweat, when I finally walk up to the house. Dad is outside, working in the flower beds along one side. I can see him from two doors down. I sneak around the other side and in through the back door. Mom is busy in the kitchen making dinner. She turns and looks at me and starts to turn back. Then she snaps her head around.

"My God," she says, really quiet, as if someone might be listening, "you're burnt." Her eyes are puffy, like she's been crying.

"Mom, look," I say, crossing the kitchen and heading down the hall, "what I am is really tired. I'm going to lie down for a while."

I slip into my room and lie down on the bed. My head

is pounding and my skin feels like dried leather. But none of that matters. Even my concern for Frank seems small. Sally is going to meet me at the beach next Saturday and, for these few moments at least, everything is right with the world.

Chapter 11

June 23, 1968
Tan Son Nhut

Jimmy,

Greetings from the bottom of the world. They finally let us have some R and R. Two weeks in Australia. I planned to do everything in Sydney: party, beach, women. It was raining when we got in, so it was hard to get a feel for the city as the bus from the airport wove in and out of traffic. All I could really see were blurry buildings and cars rushing everywhere.

I would like to tell you I hung with friends— and I did in a way, buddies from my unit and others on the base—but I haven't gotten close to anyone since Tom cashed it in. We wound up at a cheap hotel not far from downtown. Ten bucks a night. I was completely ragged, but I decided to get cleaned up and find a bar.

I found this little bar called Domingo on a street just a few blocks from the hotel. Inside, the place was jammed with men in tee shirts and women in tank tops. The jukebox was blaring Elvis. Man, I fly nine thousand miles to a war, then a couple thousand to another continent, and what do I find when I walk into a bar: Elvis.

The bartender brought me a Foster's in a frosted mug, and I thought about the warm cans of beer we put up with most of the time in Nam. I asked him about the beach, a way to get there, what was going on, any surfing, and all that, and he pulled a little plastic bag out of his shirt pocket.

"You want something really nice, I got it."

I'm soul tired of the heroin, the partying, the sense of my life isn't my own anymore. Tired of blurring the edges of my life until nothing is clear. And I'm scared, Jimmy. Scared. But the next thing I knew, I was handing him the money.

I was helpless. Everything was suddenly empty. I wanted to feel the tug of the waves, the way the swells will float you up then drop you down, and then the knowledge that a big set is coming in. I could remember, as I sat there, how good it feels to catch the hard face of a wave before it crests, then to curl up and ride the tube. I remembered how the salt water dried in my hair, how the wet suit felt like a second skin pulled up against my body. I remembered everything, Jimmy, but all I could think about was the smack in my pocket. I didn't know how it had happened.

Then I walked as fast as I could back to my room. Everything I had wanted to do in Sydney had become second-rate. The only thing that mattered was to get that buzz. I got back in and locked the door, and the only time I came out for the next ten days was to find that bartender and score again.

Why am I telling you this? I don't know. I'm amazed. That's it. I'm amazed. Two weeks in Australia and all I remember is the bartender who sold me smack.

Frank

∧

Jimmy,

They finally did it. They put me in a tunnel. We were camped somewhere deep in the mountains and had just been sitting there for two days. I had the shakes. I needed to get high, so I managed to get off in the jungle a little ways and shoot up. By the time things started moving in the camp, I was nodding out. I guess the patrol had found this tunnel not a hundred yards from where we were camped, and there was some sign it had been used recently.

The lieutenant knows what is going on with me and would bust me out of the platoon except it takes too long to get replacements, so he just rides my ass. Gets me up in the middle of the night to clean my gun, orders me up at dawn when he knows I'm jonesing and can hardly move. Well, this time, he finds me leaning up against a tree, my eyes half closed, my mouth dragging air, and he yanks me up.

"You, Staples!" he yells. "You got tunnel duty."

I managed to stand up, but it was tough. My body was numb. My head was floating like a balloon. Somehow, though, I grabbed my rifle and followed him out of camp. I must have been too high to care, because I just jumped right in.

For a minute, I could see the light behind me where the tunnel opened into the jungle, but then the blackness closed around me like night. I pulled my flashlight off my belt and pushed the button up. It wasn't much light, but I could see a few feet ahead. There were places where I could almost sit up, but mostly I had to crawl along on my belly. I was moving slow. The smack was pumping through me and my hands felt like lead, but I knew I had to keep going.

Then it happened. I thought about Todd and panic took hold. Jimmy, I pissed my pants. I have never been so scared. I promised God I'd never touch heroin again. I promised Him I'd fix things with Dad. I promised I would make sure you didn't make the mistakes I've made. Anything just to get out of there alive.

I crawled along for maybe five minutes. It's kind of hard to tell, high as I was. It might have been a half-hour. At one point I came across a place that had been dug wider, and I could see where someone had stopped and smoked a cigarette and eaten something. Right there, as if it was the end of the world and nothing would ever matter again, I curled up into the curved back of the

dirt wall and pulled my legs up against my chest. I
don't know how long I was in there, Jimmy. It
might have been an hour. It could have been days,
although I know it wasn't.

I lay there, shaking uncontrollably. After a while,
I started to calm down a bit, but by then the flashlight had dimmed. I thought about Dante's circles
of hell and I knew I'd gone all the way down. I
freaked out when I realized I couldn't remember
which way I'd come in, but I started crawling
anyway, sure I was as good as dead no matter
what. I pushed myself along, one hand out, then
the other, then I'd drag my knees up and start
over.

I don't know what it was, but something moved
in that tunnel. It moved and it ran right by me. It
had to be a rat or some damned monkey checking
out the dark insides of the jungle of sweetness and
light, but whatever it was, my heart damn near
exploded. I sat back and pulled my rifle up and
aimed where it had gone and started shooting. I
shot off everything in the clip, then sat back
again, no tears this time, no nothing.

I'd probably still be there, comatose or dead,
but after a few minutes I heard a voice. It was
the lieutenant. He was right next to me, with his
flashlight aimed straight into my eyes.

"Goddamn it, Staples," he growled, "what the hell do you think you're doing?"

I looked at him, by now so calm I could have stood in a roomful of bees and not gotten stung.

"Getting a tan," I said.

I've got a buddy named Brown in the unit. He used to do smack but doesn't anymore. He says he kicked his habit, and if I want to kick he can help.

Brown sat up with me that night. After the junk wore off I started shaking and I couldn't stop. This guy—a black guy about 250 pounds—wrapped me in his arms like I was a baby. He held me and I cried. I didn't care that I was crying.

Jimmy, I went down to the dark, deep center of it all and lived to come back out. The part of me that was supposed to die down there was numb, but the part of me that's always wanted to live was tingling at every nerve end. I lay there in that man's arms and let the world melt away, all the pain, the fear, the hunger, and I cried because I must have known right then that going down into the earth was more than doing my job. It was facing down the darkness that has filled me since I got here.

I don't know what's going to happen. Sometimes I feel strong, others I feel like this jungle's

*going to smother me. It's been two weeks, and I
haven't touched the shit. But I'm hurting, Jimmy,
and I don't know if I'm strong enough to stay
away from it.*

                Frank

                ⅄

It's early morning when I wake up and realize I never
made it for dinner last night. I get up on my knees in bed
and look out the window. The street is still, the sun just
barely poking through the hibiscus bushes Dad planted
in a landscaped island out front. I lie back down and
think about Sally, trying to piece together every second
of yesterday. I remember how she looked, standing there
above me when I first opened my eyes, how her voice
sounds when she teases Terry, how it sounds when she
talks about her brother John and the protest rallies. And
I remember her eyes, the way the sunlight sparks in them
and makes me dizzy.

   Then my thoughts return to Frank, and the good feeling in my head fades. His last few letters keep running
around in my head like a bad dream. If he were here
right now, I could talk to him about this, ask him how
I'm supposed to feel. But then, I don't know if *he* knows
anymore.

   By now the sun is trickling in my window. It's Sunday

and Mom and Dad are still asleep. I throw the covers off and sit up. For the first time I really notice how badly I got burned yesterday; it feels like someone skinned me, then poured salt all over my body. Carefully, I pull on my jeans, stiff again and rough against my skin, and dig around in my dresser drawer until I find a tee-shirt that's clean. I know my feet won't put up with another day like yesterday, so I grab some socks and my boots from the closet and go outside. I don't know exactly what I'm going to do, but I need to get away, to be by myself.

I remember the times Frank and I would drive in his old Ford out to Loxahatchee. It's part of the Everglades that has been turned into a park, where you can walk out through some of it on wooden walkways, or wander along dirt levees out to where it gradually turns wild. Frank liked to come out to listen to the alligators holler. At dusk, we'd stand along the levee, watching egrets and great blue herons wading in the shallow water around small islands in the swamp.

Sometimes you could see the gators lounging in their pools, deep places they dig with their tails so they can hang out waiting for food to swim or fly along. But you don't usually see the whole gator; what you see is two bulging eyes and two round nostrils poking out of the water. They can sit motionless like that for hours, and then, if a fish swims too close or a bird makes the mistake of landing on a mound of grass along the shore—

113

whoosh, that gator moves like lightning, its big jaws opening and closing on the unsuspecting dinner.

A couple months before he left, Frank took me out there on a Saturday morning. He'd been out with Susan the night before, and I think they'd had a fight. I could tell he was sad, but he didn't want to talk about it.

At breakfast, Mom crouched low over coffee and the paper. Dad was still asleep.

"Let's drive out to Loxahatchee," Frank said. "I want to show you something."

We managed to get out of the house before Dad woke up. It was probably eight-thirty or nine, and the sun was big and heavy in the sky. We drove out west, through Palm Beach Gardens, passing the few remaining farms, where cows stood swishing their tails at flies, munching steadily. At 441 we turned left and headed south. Already a few plots of land had been cleared, and some houses were going up, but for the most part, it was all deep country. Pine savannas spread out in all directions, with scrub palmetto and twisted, little oak trees scattered here and there. At one point, where there had been a fire the year before, I remember seeing a golden eagle perched way up in the scorched branches of a dead pine, scanning the waste for anything that moved. It cocked its head toward us as we drove by, then resumed its surveillance.

We pulled into the entrance at Loxahatchee and drove down the packed-sand-and-seashell road that led into the reserve. The road was built on a raised levee sucked up from the swamp and shored with massive chunks of coral. I like the sound of tires crunching against the seashells and gravel, so I just closed my eyes and listened.

When we stopped and parked, I opened my eyes. This was not the place Dad usually brings us. In fact, it didn't look like part of the park at all. Frank had turned somewhere off the main road coming in and driven back into the swamp away from the main parking lot. The first things I noticed when we got out were bottles and McDonald's bags strewn everywhere.

"This is where we come to party," Frank said. "We found something out here last night. Come on."

I followed him out of the clearing toward a path that disappeared a few feet into the tall grass. We walked maybe five minutes before the ground started getting soft. Flies were buzzing around my ears, and far off I could hear an airboat, its engine whining, skimming over the swamp. There was a smell out here too, increasingly pungent and very unpleasant. I had visions of a corpse, some old man who'd fallen into the swamp, washed ashore, and swollen in the sun. My mind was busy working overtime on that one, and I was wondering, too, why Frank would bring me out to show me rather than call the cops.

By now the stench was something solid. The flies were so thick I had to wave my hand in front of my mouth to keep from swallowing them. Frank had stopped just ahead and stood there looking off to his right. He was pushing the grass back with a stick he'd picked up from the ground.

"Come here," he was saying. "Look."

I came up next to him and looked back into the opening he'd made in the grass. There, like something from a late-night movie, lay the biggest alligator I have ever seen, dead and sprawled in the shallow water.

Chapter 12

Jimmy,

Night patrol is the worst. We lie low all day, sleeping in the heat, waiting for the sun to go down so we can mobilize and head into the bush. Out there, when the sky is black and the stars are so dim you can hardly see them, we move like ghosts, drifting from one dark place to another.

I'm having more and more trouble just getting going. Sometimes I think I'm losing my mind. The other guys have trouble too, but when it comes right down to it, they oil their weapons, polish their boots, and jump to attention. Lieutenant says, "Go get 'em," and they go get 'em. Me, I stand there looking stupid. Lieutenant says, "Move out," something sick and heavy rises in my stomach. I do what I'm supposed to, but I can't get it out of my head that what I'm doing is wrong. What we're doing is wrong. And on top of all of it is the smack, like the devil, running my life.

We hear on the army news that the kids at home are protesting the war. Some of the guys who've finished their tours and gone home have written back to tell us college students were throwing trash and spitting at them as they got off planes. Some of the ones still here, and the ones just in country for the first time, talk about national pride and how the hippies should all cut their hair and come to Nam for a year, like that would somehow cure them.

I don't know. I find myself on the side of those college kids. Not that grunts like me deserve scorn for all this—it's not our fault—but if I had stayed home, I know I'd be in California now, living with some buddies, marching in the streets. But I don't have much time to think about it. A few of us get together and talk, knowing we'll be out in a few months, about what we're going to do when we get home, and almost everyone but me is sure. One guy says he's going to college—wants to get a job in business. Another one is going back to his family's farm in Iowa. Another one is getting married the day he gets back.

Me? I don't have a clue. Only six months of duty to go and I can't think of anything but coming home and going to sleep. Sometimes I even think it would be better if I got killed over here. It would save everybody at home a lot of trouble. Mostly, I wouldn't have to live inside this head of mine with its awful wants and pains. Paradise for me used to be a long day at the beach and going out with Susan. Hell, I never told her this, but I wanted to marry her. And I haven't even written her in more than six months.

I write to you and I write to Mom and Dad. Of course, you're the only one I really write to. I'm sure they show you the letters I write them. It's all just fluff. I can't tell Mom I'm sleeping in water most of the time, watching guys die like it's football on Sunday. I certainly couldn't tell her about slipping away from camp at night to get high on smack. And Dad, even if I could tell him, what would it mean? He'd just get all pissed off and tell me to get it together.

119

Or he'd swear at me and tell me I am worthless. Either way, there's not much shoulder there to cry on. Except for you. I'd never thought of it that way until just now, but maybe that's it. A little weird, don't you think, that I lean on my little brother for support? Maybe somehow I think of you as innocent and I want you to stay that way. Maybe if I tell you how awful the world really is, you'll be more careful.

Tomorrow we move out again, this time back to Pleiku, up in the mountains. I almost wish we'd stay in the Delta. Even with the rain and the endless mud, at least it's flat. At Pleiku, the jungle's as thick, but we struggle all day long just to get to the top of a hill, and then we walk back down and find another one to climb the next day. The worst part is when we run across the VC. Then we fight for hours just to move a few feet up that hill. It sometimes takes days to get to the top. And when we're done, we move on and the VC get the hill back like nothing ever happened. It's crazy.

Lately, I've been reading whatever I can get my hands on. It keeps my mind off the war: both the one on the ground here and the other one in my body. I've got leave in Saigon again soon, and I am scared to go. Scared not to go too. I know I'll walk the street until I find some boy who's got those little plastic bags, ten bucks a pop, and I'll hide out in a cheap hotel until it's time to get back to the unit. Sometimes I actually find myself wishing I could just stay here and wander off into the jungle with a gun and two weeks' rations, stay away from Saigon, safe from temptation.

I know there's no excuse for any of this. I can tell you it's the war, but that's bullshit. Other guys suffer without the need to nod out every leave. I mean, everyone smokes pot, but that seems so innocent to me now, almost like drinking milk. Maybe I've really kicked it. Maybe when I'm home the need will just evaporate, and I'll get a normal job and forget the war. Maybe.

Frank

∧

August 18, 1968
Tan Son Nhut

Jimmy,
Did I ever tell you about the women in Saigon? I probably didn't because I was wasted most of

the time. *Well, they're beautiful. So thin and small you think they're little girls, but they're grown-up everywhere. The sad thing is they stand on the street and hang out in bars and sell themselves for next to nothing.*

This last weekend, we went in for some R and R and were drinking in a little bar when the guys kind of circled and started teasing me because I'd never, you know, bought a girl. Right there, they took up a collection and paid a pretty girl with big, black eyes and hair down to her waist. One of them led her over to me, nodding to her as they walked, whispering something in her ear. She laughed. When they got to where I was sitting, she smiled and reached for my hand, rubbed it, and ran one finger up and down on the back of it.

"You come with me?"

Her voice was like fog on an early morning at the beach. I had to go with her. I'd never live it down if I didn't, so I got up and we left the bar. Even though it was ten at night, the air was sticky. Up and down the street, people moved slowly, looking in windows, some of them disappearing into dark doorways. It was only a block, but I struggled with myself more in that one block than I have in eighteen years and thousands of miles.

At a dingy storefront, she stopped and fumbled

in her purse. She pulled out a key and put it into the lock of the front door.

"My father store," she explained.

We went in, and in the very back there was a couch and a mattress on the floor. She lit some candles, then offered me a beer and told me I could stay with her all night, until dawn when her father would get up and come downstairs. I don't think he knew what she was doing down there at night.

I opened the beer and took a long swig, watching her move around the little room at the back of the shop, straightening things up. When she started to pull her shirt up over her head, I told her to stop.

"Why stop?" she asked, amazed, I think, that I would say it.

And then I started blurting out the whole thing. I told her about Susan and about heroin and about getting my life back. I told her about you and how I had to get back to Florida so we could surf. I told her about Dad and Mom and all the bullshit we put up with. We sat there until just before the sun came up, Jimmy, and I talked to her, that's all. I talked and she listened. I don't know how much she understood, but she listened. I don't know how much I understood, but I talked.

When I hooked back up with my buddies that morning, they punched me on the shoulder and said, "Welcome back to manhood, little boy."

I didn't tell them what really happened. Jimmy, am I nuts? Wouldn't any guy want her to take her shirt off, everything? But I've got to tell you, just sitting there that night—the sound of an old electric fan whirring from the window, cars passing on the street that seemed a million miles away, her quiet face turned toward me, listening—was the sweetest thing I've had in Nam.

And the best part? I made it through my leave without the smack.

Frank

⌄

"You see that, Jimmy?"

Frank was standing aside to give me a better view of the dead gator.

"Not so scary when they're dead, huh?"

I was having trouble breathing, and my heart was banging. Right up to the last instant before I saw it, I was convinced it would be a human body. That it was instead a dead and partially decomposed alligator didn't help to calm me much.

The gator had to be fifteen feet long, maybe longer. Its eyes were gone, eaten, I imagined, by the little fresh-water crabs that pick at everything that smells this bad. Maggots crawled in and around a hole in the side of the belly. I thought I was going to be sick, but it was still fascinating. I moved closer. Frank pushed a stick into the soft skin and an army of bugs came rushing out.

"Pretty cool, huh?" he said, leaning on the stick and watching the swollen sides of the gator begin to shrink as the air inside escaped with the bugs.

Frank wasn't usually one to be fascinated with dead things, so I was trying to get my bearings, to figure out what he was up to. The air around us felt clammy and thick. Flies buzzed in dense clouds around my face.

"The biggest thing in the swamp," he said, "and when it's dead, everything else has a feast."

We hung out at Loxahatchee for most of the morning, hiking out to the observation tower, where you could climb up and see everything for miles, marshy flats in all directions, dotted with cypress domes and hammocks. As the day grew hotter, things got quiet, birds stopped circling and swooping in for snacks. Once in a while, a heron would lift itself up on its long, feathery wings and flap from one muddy bank to another and then settle down as motionless as it had been before it flew.

Frank had brought some apples and a big bottle of

Coke. We sat there in the shade of the rough wood roof of the tower and ate.

"Do you ever think about growing up and getting out of here?" he asked me.

He was seventeen and only months away from graduating. I told him no, and it was the truth. I really didn't think that far ahead. I was fourteen and just starting to think about what it meant to be in high school next year.

"Jimmy," he said, "I think about it all the time, but I can't decide what it is I want to do."

That's when he first talked about Haight-Ashbury. It wasn't the big mecca it is now, but there were stories. There was a band called the Grateful Dead that threw wild parties, a group of weirdoes who called themselves the Merry Pranksters, and some guy named Owsley who was making LSD in his basement and handing it out for free. All of that stuff sounded scary to me. I was curious, but the idea of actually doing it was enough to make me shiver. Frank wanted to go.

"Anything," he said, "to get away from Dad."

An air force jet screamed over us, so low I felt the sound as something physical. When the noise died down, Frank looked at me, and it was the strangest look I've ever seen.

"Or," he said, "I could go to Vietnam."

Driving back, we were quiet. I watched the landscape

change from swamp to dry savannah to grassy subdivisions, where men were outside in shorts mowing lawns and kids were riding bikes in the streets. I thought about the alligator, how its body stunk, and for a minute had a flash of war the way it looked on Cronkite.

Chapter 13

August 28, 1968
Tan Son Nhut

Jimmy,

You must be getting ready to go back to school. Palm Beach Gardens High seems like another life. Almost as if I've been turned inside out and who I used to be has dried up like scraps of paper that catch in the wind and blow away. I can't even get your image straight in my head anymore. Worse, I can't get an image of myself straight either.

I've only got a few months left to go. I don't know if I'm more afraid of getting hit before I leave or of coming home. Things will never be the same. I think about getting my old board out of the garage and waxing it and heading over to Singer Island, driving down A1A like I'd never left. I think about calling Susan, though I don't know if she'd even want to talk to me after all these months with no letters, no call, no anything. I think about going out to the swamp with you, plinking frogs with my old .22. I even think about trying to get along with Dad. It's not him anymore I can't stand; it's me.

You know, what's weird is that I always thought of myself as pretty smart and capable of anything I wanted to do. And I thought Dad was just a bastard, an angry, drunken bastard. But now I don't know what to think. Maybe Dad has something burning up inside of him that makes him drink and yell. I think there's a kind of anger and fear so deep that once it gets inside of you, there's nothing you can ever do to shake it. I don't want to be like that, Jimmy, but I'm afraid I am.

I've had some luck staying away from smack, but I don't know how long it will last. I managed to get a weekend in Saigon and watched movies, ate in restaurants, and hung out with some buddies. No girls this time. I can't say I had much fun, since most of the time I was craving a buzz.

The whole world seems hollow without it. I

promised if I could get through two days without it I'd let myself have just a little bit. But I got to the end of the two days and realized a little bit would never do it, and so I didn't let myself have any. I was shaking and sweaty by the time we got back.

I still can't quite imagine doing anything normal. What's normal, anyway? Surfing, dating, getting a job . . . it all sounds so pointless in the face of everything I've seen over here. I feel kind of like the Amaryllis, *stuck with my nose in the sand. Is that damned ship still there? I mean, shouldn't it be out there sailing around, lugging stuff from one port to another? That's me. I could be going somewhere in life, but instead, I'm stuck in a country so far from home the only things that remind me it's still the planet earth are the blood, the sweat, the smell of gasoline and napalm.*

Frank

⌒

It's hard to believe Frank's been gone more than a year. Hard to believe I'm back at school, drifting from class to class, reading textbooks about history, studying war. Frank's letters still come, but they're not as frequent now. Sometimes they are hopeful, but mostly pretty depressed.

Once in a while I get one that just sounds mad, and then I think maybe Frank is going to be okay.

Susan called last week. She wanted to know if we'd heard anything. Mom answered the phone, and all she could pass along was the meaningless drivel that Frank writes to them. Basically, the way they see it, he is fighting the war and counting the days, and no, he hasn't said anything about Susan. Hasn't he written? Well, that's too bad. Maybe Susan could write to him again herself and ask. Mom sat there quietly for a long time after they hung up.

I know I should mind my own business, but I went back to my room and dug through my desk until I found Susan's phone number. When she answered the phone, it was awkward, but I pushed on.

"Susan, listen," I said, trying not to sound too young and goofy. "This is Jimmy. I need to talk to you about Frank. He'd kill me, but this is important."

We agreed to meet at the Dunkin' Donuts after school the next day.

⋏

The day dragged on forever, but when the bell rang after eighth period, I started to feel panicky. I had no idea what I was going to say. *Hi, Susan. Frank's a junkie, but he still loves you; he just hates himself.* Nothing I came up with made any sense, but I had called Sally after I got off the phone with Susan and she said I was doing the right thing.

I'd been hanging out with Sally for a couple of months, and she hadn't lost even a little bit of her edge. She was always direct and never once did anything stupid or immature. I felt like I'd found a best friend. She offered to meet us at the donut shop, but I told her I needed to do this alone.

When I walked in, the sweet smell of donuts and hot oil filled my nostrils. I thought I was going to be sick. I sat down next to Susan and ordered a cup of coffee before I could even look in her eyes.

"What's going on?" she asked.

She was sitting hunched over on the round stool and spun around toward me as she talked. I had forgotten how pretty Susan is, and for a minute, I was so nervous I couldn't say a thing.

"Frank's had a rough time," I told her. "The war is hard on him. I mean, it's hard on everyone, but he doesn't handle it very well. Did he tell you when he was wounded?"

She nodded her head. "That's pretty much the last time I heard from him," she said. "Six months ago."

I swallowed a mouthful of coffee too fast, burning the back of my throat. I grabbed some ice water and took a big drink before I could go on. But once I started talking, there was no way to shut me up. I had told Sally everything, but she didn't know Frank. This was different. Susan knew Frank almost as well as I did, or at least I imagined she did. I told her about the morphine and the trips to Saigon that followed. I told her about Australia and the battles Frank described. I told her about how scared he was to come home and that he loved her but didn't think she'd want him anymore. She started crying, and I could feel my own eyes getting wet. The waitress came over and poured more coffee. I ordered a couple of eclairs, one for Susan and one for me.

"I feel like I should write him," Susan said.

"Maybe hearing from you will give him something to hang on to."

"I don't even know what I'd *say*," she continued.

She was drumming her fingers on the countertop. Outside, afternoon traffic rushed by.

"Please don't tell him I talked to you," I said.

Chapter 14

September 15, 1968
Tan Son Nhut

Jimmy,

The days have started to get longer and longer. I sometimes wonder how I'll hold out until my discharge. Everything sort of melts into everything else over here. Today the sun is clouded over and the air is not its usual sticky self. I have been sitting in front of my barracks on the base for two hours, listening to Armed Forces Radio.

We lost a couple of guys on this last mission. Generally, I can't even remember their names for more than a few days after they're gone. Except this time. Brown and Hernandez. Brown and Hernandez. I keep repeating their names. It'll make them last a little longer. These guys were some of the best friends I've had. I mean, we didn't hang together much except in the field, but out there . . . well, out there is where it really counts. I think that's what I liked about them both; they were loners too. On base, they stayed to themselves like I do. But in the field, they would do anything to help one of the rest of us.

On leave too, they have been there for me. I think I told you about Brown. He had his own problems with smack and kicked it because it was making him crazy. Always wanting more, getting it, nodding out for days, then coming back to the surface of this filthy world and wanting still more. That's not really how he put it, but that's how I feel. Anyway, he hung with me the last few times we went into Saigon, and he helped me stay clean.

The first time we went in after I'd decided to kick, it was the middle of the afternoon and the streets were filled with carts and people selling vegetables. Cars whipped by, honking wildly. A couple of the guys who usually sold the stuff recognized me and came right up to me on the street. Brown came up beside me and grabbed my hand just as I was reaching for my wallet. At first, the dealer thought he was trying to rob me and he started to yell for his friends. Brown gave him one nasty look and the guy just backed off. I guess the sight of a 250-pound black man in uniform staring him down was more than he wanted to mess with.

I was pretty bummed out. I made a lot of noise about doing what I wanted and no badass would stop me, but Brown stood his ground. He led me to a corner restaurant and ordered two Cokes. Then he told me his story. Jimmy, it was worse than anything you can imagine. He signed up for the same reason I did: to get away from home. Only his home has ours beat hands down.

His dad whipped him from before he can remember. His mom worked two jobs, but it was never enough for them to live on. There are only the three of them, but his dad could never find a job that suited him and after a while quit looking. Then it got really bad. Drinking and drugs, other women his dad brought home. Times he watched his dad hit his mom so hard she passed out and couldn't go to work for a few days because of bruises. Well, you get the picture.

He wound up in country with a bellyful of anger like nobody's business, and started shooting smack the first month he was here. But he watched *a couple friends go down, out in the field so high they didn't know their names, and he decided he wanted to live. He said sometimes he wanted to get high again more than he knew what to do with, but he would think about his mother and a girlfriend back home, and it was enough to keep him strong and clean.*

I'm trying, Jimmy, to be that strong too. In a way, I owe it to him, being straight and clean and doing something good in this life. I owe it to Brown and all the others who bought it over here.

Just another couple months now and I'm done. One more mission next week, then some R and R. I'm counting minutes.

Frank

Chapter 15

The letter came last night.

Dear Mr. and Mrs. Staples, your son, Frank, did not return from a mission in Southeast Asia and is presumed missing in action. . . .

I didn't actually read it; I didn't need to. Dad's face went white. The sheet of paper trembled in his hands. Mom put her hands up to her face and started sobbing.

Chapter 16

This morning I'm going through the motions: opening my bedroom door, stepping out into the hallway, shuffling down the hall toward the bathroom, washing my face and brushing my teeth, staring hard into the mirror. As I dress for school, I can hear my parents in their bedroom. No words, just Mom crying and Dad pacing back and forth.

My hands feel as if all the muscles in them have gone on strike. I try to button my shirt but can't get it right. The light, coming in through the window, is gray and dirty. I pull the blinds back, and everything outside looks bleak, the palms drooping in a light drizzle, cars creeping down the street like they're lost. Somehow, I manage to pull on my sneakers.

Just as I step out of my room, Dad comes out of the bedroom and sort of slumps down the hall. I follow him into the kitchen, but he doesn't even notice I'm there.

"Good morning," I whisper.

He turns to look at me and lift his hands, palms up, then drops them back to his side.

"Good morning, son."

My mother doesn't come out, so I scrounge in the cupboard until I find a box of cereal, grab the milk from the refrigerator and two clean bowls from the drain board in the sink, and set everything on the table. Dad is standing at the window with his back to me.

"You hungry?" I ask him.

Nothing.

From the end of the hall, I can hear Mom crying. I eat my cereal in silence and go outside to catch the bus.

Riding the bus to school, I'm numb. None of this looks right anymore. The other kids are talking and laughing, but their conversations and laughter are miles away. When we get to Lake Park, Terry gets on the bus and moves down the aisle until he finds me, then sits down.

"Hey, man, how you doing?"

"Huh?" I ask, not really knowing if my mouth is going to work or not.

"Man, I can't believe my old man," he says. "Last night, he came into my room and handed me a book. It's this thing about finding yourself and making peace with something inside you. Weird. I don't get it. Half the time he doesn't pay any attention to me, then out of the blue he wants to help me find myself."

"What did you do with it?" I ask him numbly.

"What?" he asks.

"The book."

"I started to read it, but it was pretty boring. I'll probably stick it on my shelf until he forgets."

"Listen," I finally say, "Frank's gone. Missing in action. We got a letter last night."

It's like I hit him or something. He sits back in his seat and stares at me.

"Hey, Jimmy, I didn't know. I'm sorry."

"Yeah," I say, then lean back and close my eyes.

For the rest of the ride, I just tune out, thinking. When Frank left, something drained away from the whole family. Dad never seemed to want him around, but once Frank was gone, he'd gotten more and more quiet, working in the yard, or turning on the TV and tuning Mom and me out. Mom seemed just plain lost a lot of the time. She'd cook dinner and set the table for four instead of three. She'd go into Frank's room and peel back the sheets and throw them in the laundry, even though no one had slept in them for months. As for me, well, I'd gone on pretty much as always.

I stare out the window of the bus. The sky is heavy now with black clouds, the misty rain from this morning beginning to fall in sheets. The way rain fell on Frank in Nam. I see mothers loading little kids in station wagons, and I think about village women rounding up their kids when Frank and his unit swept through. One kid stumbles as her mother tries to help her into a car, and she falls facedown in a pool of water. Her mother grabs her hard by the sleeve of her jacket and yanks her up. The mother begins to scream at the little girl, who is soaking wet and crying. *So this is the World,* I think.

The bus pulls up in the wide half-circle in front of the school. I get off without saying anything to Terry and push through the groups of kids standing around outside waiting for the first bell. Moving now in a kind of a blur, I head straight for the library.

I'm tearing through the resource section when Mrs. Nevers comes in.

"What are you doing, Jimmy?" she asks, the tone of her voice just this side of pissed off.

I don't answer, so she repeats herself, this time louder and edgier. When I turn to look at her, I can't hold it back anymore and I just start crying. I don't do it on purpose—the last thing in the world I want is pity from Mrs. Nevers—but she softens immediately and comes over to where I'm sitting on the floor with geography books scattered around me.

"What is it?" she says, and puts a hand on my shoulder.

I try to say it, but I can't. I open my mouth, but nothing comes out. I can feel myself slump, my shoulders falling forward, and then I just sit there.

Finally, when I catch my breath and can speak, I say, "I want to find out where Frank is. That's all. I just want to find my brother."

The principal calls my mother. When she pulls up in front of the school, I gather my things and step outside. The air is sticky. She gets out of the car and puts her arms around me. I can feel her breath on my neck. She's crying.

"You seemed so strong, we just didn't think . . ."

Her voice trails off.

You never think, that's the problem, I'm saying to myself, over and over. *You never think.*

Everything outside loses focus. I'm mad now. Mad at Mom and Dad, mad at school and all my friends who don't have brothers over there in Nam, mad at the United States for picking on some little country in Southeast Asia, then sending Frank over to die for it. And I'm mad at Frank.

"Goddamn it," I say.

I have never sworn in front of my mother. She looks at me, a nervous, startled look in her eyes.

"Goddamn it," I repeat.

When we get home, I go into my room and sit down on the bed. I don't know what to do. I pull Frank's letters out from under the bed, where I've hidden them with old model airplanes and cars. For a long time, I just look at them, a pile impressive for its thickness, maybe three inches. Three inches of letters in a year. How many pages to an inch? Perhaps fifty? How many words to a page? Handwritten, probably not more than a hundred. So everything Frank has been for the last year is reduced to maybe fifteen thousand words.

I sit until the shadows fill the room. When I hear Dad come in, I go out into the living room. I'm waiting there when he rounds the corner. He sees me, stops, then gets a funny look on his face. It's like he's frozen, stunned by what he knows is coming.

"It's all your fault," I say, my voice as low and even as it's ever been, and turn back to my room.

He doesn't follow me. He doesn't even say anything, but I hear him drop into his big chair in the living room. Mom is in the kitchen clinking pans and dishes, but I'm not hungry. I lie down on my bed and put my hands behind my head. Little by little, the light fades, and I drift off.

In the morning, I get up and dress for school, grab another bowl of Cheerios, and am almost out the door when Dad comes out of his bedroom and calls me.

"Junior," he says quietly, "you're right."

Then he turns and walks down the hall to his room and closes the door after him.

Chapter 17

I walk down the hall and stand there in front of my parents' bedroom door. Inside, I hear my father restlessly moving around, rustling through the closet, then I hear the creak of the bed, his weight settling in. My mother's voice is too soft to understand. His voice, low and breaking, rises for a moment. A few clear words emerge from the blur of their conversation.

". . . nothing we can do . . ."

"God, it can't be true. . . ."

"Maybe they'll find . . ."

Then their voices grow quiet again and I can't understand anything more that they say.

I go back to my room, hurrying now so I can leave before they come out. I pull the boxes out from under my bed, take my books out of my backpack, and put Frank's letters in. The light is coming through the blinds in narrow bands, making bars across the wall. It's more a feeling than a thought, but I think of Frank — squatting somewhere in a cage, starving, being tortured and beaten — and a pain shoots through my head, like a headache, but not a headache. Something else.

Outside, the air is cool. Autumn in Florida is not really autumn, but we do get some cool days. Almost never the kind of cool that makes you shiver, but it's a nice relief from the sweaty hot of summer. One thing about autumn is the waves. This time of year the big waves roll in, set after set, day after day.

Instead of catching the bus, I walk up to Federal and head south. I think about the cops catching me playing hooky, but I don't care. Somehow the whole idea of breaking their stupid school attendance rule seems smaller than a speck of dust. As I pass the street that leads to Terry's house, I hesitate but go on. I could try to get him to skip school with me, but I want to be alone today.

It takes three hours, walking steady. I dodge into alleys or doorways when I see a cop car cruising down the street. Before I even cross the causeway, the smell of the ocean fills my nose, sort of fishy and rotten and sweet all at the same time. Two blocks away, I can hear the waves. I head north along A1A and walk until I see the dark shape of the *Amaryllis,* like a shadow lifting up from the shore. Finding the hollow in the dune where Terry and I hung out the day I first connected with Sally, I stop and pull my pack off my back. I think about Sally and wonder what she'll say when I tell her. I know she already wonders why I didn't call her last night. But I will. I will.

The wind from the ocean pushes against me, blowing my hair straight back. Grains of sand the wind picks up and carries sting my face and hands. The ship just sits there, dark and imposing. Huge patches of rust spread out along the hull. In the paper yesterday, I read that they are getting ready to pull it out of here this winter to sink it offshore. And I panicked, thinking Frank will never see it, never surf in its shadow again. I sit down hard and lay my head against my pack. After a few minutes, I sit up, reach inside, and pull the letters out.

All morning, I lean into the dune. Slowly, the sun crawls up until finally it starts to warm me. Even then, I feel cold. I pull letters out at random, not caring if they're good ones or bad ones. It's like I feel the full press of Frank's entire time in Nam as one awful sweep. Almost as if it doesn't matter if he is wounded or whole, addicted to heroin or clean, coming home or missing.

A seagull glides down and lands in front of me. It puts its legs out like it expects to skid, but flaps its wings at the last instant and comes down without stirring up a grain of sand. It struts around like it owns the place.

I reach into my pack and feel around until I find my lunch bag, open it, and pull my sandwich out. Absently, I pick it into pieces and toss them to the gull. It hops around and snaps them up, watching me as it gulps and swallows.

Out past the lines of waves, a ship moves slowly north. A thread of black smoke trails up in a long arc behind it. By now the sun is almost overhead and the sand is starting to feel warm. The *Amaryllis* casts no shadow.

I study the hard lines of the ship, jutting out 450 feet into the Atlantic. Waves break past the stern and roll toward shore in even sets. The sky is gray, streaked with wispy, orange clouds that stretch across the horizon.

⌒

I remember one day in particular that Frank and I came out here. We both had boards; I'd just gotten mine the night before, and Frank came into my room the next morning and shook me. It wasn't even light yet, but he was dressed and ready.

"Come on, Jimmy," he said. I rubbed my eyes and glared at him. "There's waves out there and time's a wastin'," he said, pulling the sheets off me.

It was still dark when we finished loading the boards on the rack he'd built for the top of his car. I got in the passenger side, and Frank climbed in behind the wheel. He pulled a joint from behind his ear and waved it under my nose.

"Come on, Jimmy. Time to celebrate," he said.

As always, I made my excuses, and finally he fired it up and smoked it in silence as we headed down Federal.

We stopped at the Dunkin' Donuts and he ordered two cups of black coffee, pushing one toward me when the waitress brought them over.

"Cream's for wimps," he said, and started sipping his, the steam like smoke rising up into his dark hair.

I think I knew right then that Frank was leaving. He'd be out of school in a few weeks, and the tension with Dad had done nothing but escalate.

As if he were reading my mind, he leaned over to me like he was going to tell me a secret.

"Jimmy," he said, "I won't be here forever, man. You should cut loose and party with me before I'm gone."

I watched him then, as he turned back to his coffee, a smile on his face, the early sun just starting to come in through the windows shimmering on his cheek.

"You still thinking about San Francisco?" I asked.

"Who knows?" he said.

The beach was more beautiful that morning than I've ever seen it, stretched like a sleeping cat in the light of the rising sun. When we stepped out on the sand, the animal that lives in the world started to wake up, and by the time we were paddling out over the first line of swells, we both could feel a pulse, like something beating in us, driving us out on the sea.

I had gotten to the point where I really didn't notice the *Amaryllis* anymore; like anything that's always just there, it had become invisible. But that morning there was something about it that made me stop and look at it for a long minute. Frank was twenty feet away, sitting on his board, brushing his hair out of his eyes. He turned to look too.

"Kind of like a nightmare, huh?" he said, turning toward me. "Imagine walking down the beach one night, the stars out like diamonds, the air a kind of sweet perfume, a beautiful girl walking along beside you, when all of a sudden, a ship the size of Rhode Island barrels out of the darkness and rams right into the sand. What would you do? Would you run? Would you piss your pants?"

I didn't answer. The slap of water against the boards, the light breeze, the feeling of sitting there on my *own* board somehow made questions like that seem kind of stupid.

"I'd stop," he said. "And I'd forget everything else until I'd gotten a feel for this thing, this monster stuck like something from another planet in my own backyard. Until you understand a thing, you can't get past it.

I kind of like the idea of things the world tosses in my path, things that interrupt the normal flow."

He was always talking like that, especially when he smoked pot. Things that didn't seem to make any sense. Usually, I just ignored him. The truth is, I have always been a little jealous that his head works like that.

Right about then, a set of waves started surging in. I paddled into position, waiting until the right one came along. I watched them breaking, the top edge curling over at a certain point, waiting for the one I knew would be *the one*. If it curled too soon, it would lose its force before I could get set on its face. If it held back too long, there was a chance it would swell and fade without ever becoming a wave. I could see them and feel them when they came, the good ones. And when the first one came that morning, I turned the board and pushed for all I was worth until I felt the force of the ocean catching me. And then I was flying, lifting myself up and standing, the solid, good feel of the board under my feet while the ocean slipped away beneath me.

∧

Now, though, after everything that's happened, I think it's more than the sea that slips away from me. I study the *Amaryllis* closely, but I'm thinking about Frank, how some damned hurricane got inside of him and blew him off course, slammed him into the coast of a beautiful, dangerous country, and locked him there, even as he was beginning to cut himself free.

"I don't agree, Frank." I mouth the words silently to myself, tears starting up in spite of my best attempts to hold them back. "I don't like the things the world has tossed in our paths."

Chapter 18

The waves roll in, big sets of five and seven, and I don't even care. It's been a month since the news. A pelican droops by, flapping his big, floppy wings, then coasting just over the water. It's late enough now that some surfers have come out after school; they're waxing their boards and pulling on wet suits. Because tonight is Halloween, three guys down the beach pull on masks when they've finished waxing their boards. One of them, a friend of Frank's I've surfed with before, sees me and waves. He adjusts a Frank Zappa mask, then walks into the water and paddles out into the surf, rising into the foamy breakers, then disappearing into the trough on the other side, then rising again.

My thoughts shake themselves loose from the inside. I've been sitting in the same place for hours, sifting through Frank's words. The sun is starting to drop behind the dunes, and my legs are so stiff they hurt when I stand up. My stomach growls. I pick up the letters and arrange them in a pile, then stuff them back in my pack. Up and down A1A, people are stepping out of hotel rooms and apartments and walking, all of them, in the same direction—toward the beach. A few cars are turning onto the highway from side streets and accelerating north and south.

I start walking, but my legs feel like they're made of putty. It occurs to me that I'm miles from home and I'm not going to be able to make it back. My thoughts are coming thick and slow now, not really mine, I think, but Frank's, maybe. I imagine he is trying to get through to me, but I shake my head, angry at myself for thinking stupid, impossible things.

Green benches line the beach, paint peeling where the wooden slats connect with heavy concrete frames, all of them facing the ocean. My legs suddenly feel too weary to support me, and I sit down.

Nowhere to go, I think, the voice in my head not quite right, not quite mine. Absently, I reach inside my pack and feel around until my fingers close around a banana I stuck in there this morning.

The faintly rotten taste of the fruit, warm and so soft

I don't even have to chew it, brings me back to my senses. The broad expanse of sand leading to the edge of the water is glittering, and shadows play across little ripples formed by wind in the last glow of the sun. A couple of old people are walking down where the sand is packed hard; they're holding hands and laughing. I get up and run at the seagulls that are flocking around scattered crumbs and bits of food. They flap their wings in a flurry of irritation and circle the spot until I go back and sit down, then they settle again to their meal.

My legs feel stronger now. I push the pack to one side of the bench and stand. Then I'm running, plowing through the deep, soft sand. Now the sand is hard and wet, and now I am in the water. When the water swirls up around my knees I dive straight into a wave just as it is cresting, and I swim as far underwater as I can before my breath gives out.

When I step out of the water, the sun is behind the buildings and the air is beginning to feel cool. I find my pack and look up and down A1A. Digging in the pocket of my jeans, I find a dime and start walking toward the Rutledge. Around back, I go straight to the pay phone that they put there for guests to call home to New York and New Jersey, and I put the dime in the slot. I have to think for a minute, then, remembering the numbers as if they're coming to me from the back of a long, hard dream, I dial home.

Mom doesn't say much as she drives. It's not really dark yet, but streetlights along Federal are coming on, and I can see Halloween decorations strung in the windows of the stores and offices. Finally, the familiar streets of North Palm swing into view, but everything looks weird. I can't figure out if it's the Halloween stuff or something else.

As we pull into the neighborhood, a group of goblins, ghosts, skeletons, and witches cross the street in front of the car and Mom slows down, then stops. A particularly nasty-looking witch reaches into her bag, turns toward us as she pulls her hand out of the bag, and heaves something straight at us. Just as the egg splats on the windshield, the kids take off running, disappearing into the yard of a house lit up with pumpkin lanterns and decked with orange-and-black crepe paper. Mom turns on the windshield wipers and pushes the squirt button, but the egg just smears on the glass.

"Damn," I hear her whisper between her teeth.

Neither of us can see out. Mom puts her hands down by her side, lowers her head, and starts to cry.

We sit there for a couple of minutes before a car pulls up behind us, flashing its bright lights and honking. Mom sort of wakes up then, and we move off slowly, up one block, then left. She's still crying when we pull into the carport and I get out of the car.

I go around to her side of the car, and open her door. She just sits there, then reaches, as if she'd never touched me before, and runs her fingers down my face.

"Mom, are you okay?"

I'm squinting in the dark to try to see her, but all I can make out is the shape of her hair piled up on her head the way she likes it. She climbs out and puts both of her arms around me, still sobbing, still saying nothing at all.

Dad's inside working on a drink.

"Hullo, Junior," he says unevenly. "How was your day?"

"I went to the beach."

"You did what?"

"I skipped school, Dad," I say impatiently.

I turn and head toward my room, flipping on the hall light as I reach the corner.

"Stop right there, young man," he says loudly.

I keep on walking. I hear my mother hurry across the room.

"Leave him alone," she says, as I close my door.

Chapter 19

It's a clear night. Stars blink across the sky like someone lighting matches. When the moon rises full above the palms behind the house, it's easy to imagine a witch on a broomstick silhouetted there. *All Hallow's Eve:* the night the dead come back to haunt the living.

All evening, trick-or-treaters ring the bell. Mom keeps a bowl of candy by the door and acts scared when she opens it to find the little ghosts and pirates standing there. I can hear her voice but not the words. It's funny how much you can tell about how someone is feeling or what they're thinking just from the tone in their voice.

By now I've read every one of Frank's letters a dozen times. But I get them out and read them again and again.

I feel like a sleuth from the CIA looking for clues to an international crime.

I haven't had the nerve to call Susan. I don't know what to say, how to tell her Frank is MIA. I've barely talked to Sally since the letter came. Two nights this week I've come home and found a message Mom had scribbled on a pad of paper by the phone saying Sally called, would I call her back? I told Mom to tell her anything if she called, just not to make me talk to her. I could see pain in Mom's eyes when I said that.

It's after ten when I finally drift to sleep.

When I wake up, it's the middle of the night. I've been dreaming about Frank. Something about his asking permission to leave and visit us. He's arguing with some officers, but they just turn away from him, and he's standing there watching something off in the distance.

He looks at me sadly and says, "Sorry, Jimmy, I tried. They just won't let me go."

The sky is clear and the stars are bright. The palm outside my window waves slowly, one frond brushing rhythmically against the house. It's so quiet, at first I think I woke up because it was too hard to be in the dream; then I notice something else. It sounds like someone laughing a long way off, but it's close, right outside. I stand up on the bed and strain my eyes to see. The yard is empty and the street is completely still.

I put on my robe and push the bedroom door open

just a little, listening. When I step into the hall, the nightlight my mother put there throws a weird shadow all along the floor. I cross the living room and slowly open the front door, careful to make as little noise as possible. The air is cooler out here, and I can smell the night-blooming jasmine Dad planted around the side of the house. Stepping out, I have to stop for a minute to let my eyes adjust to the dark. Then I see it, a dark shape hunched against the front of the house. I move closer, and the crying stops.

"Dad?" I say, reaching out to touch his shoulder.

He doesn't say anything, but he looks up at me, his face pale and distorted. I sit down next to him and put my arm over his shoulder.

"Dad," I whisper, "I didn't mean it, what I said about it being your fault."

He pulls me close and hugs me until I don't think I can breathe.

"I know it's not my fault he's disappeared, Jimmy, but I ran him off just as sure as if I packed his bags and put him on a bus."

He shifts his weight and looks away from me.

"Ever since he was little," he says, "I pushed him and pushed him. Until I pushed him away."

We sit there for a long time, listening together to the sounds of the night.

"I love you, Dad," I say.

"I love you too, son."

He squeezes my hand.

I get up and go inside, back to bed. Later, I hear the front door open and shut, then the sound of my father's footsteps padding down the hall. I can tell he stops outside my room, because the band of light along the bottom of the door is interrupted. He pauses for several moments and then gently turns the doorknob. I close my eyes as though I'm asleep. I lie so still I can hear him breathing. He moves closer to my bed, then bends over me and runs his fingers through my hair. I don't know how long he stays before he stands and turns and leaves the room. I can hear the click of his bedroom door closing and then everything is quiet.

Chapter 20

The sun is a dull glow around the edges of trees when I wake up again. After Dad left my room last night, I lay awake for a long time. When I finally fell asleep, my dreams were restless. This morning I'm tired, but there's no way I can drop off again. I throw the sheets back and stretch before I open my eyes. I already know I'm not going to school again today. I don't want to be around other people. Well, *most* other people.

I dress quickly and grab my pack, stuffing all the letters back in it. I look at the clock: it's early; Mom and Dad won't be up for at least an hour.

Traffic on Federal is thin when I stick out my thumb and wave it at the few cars that pass me by. Finally, a red Mustang pulls over and I hop in. The driver is a young guy, maybe nineteen—Frank's age. He's got long hair and a mustache that curls all the way down his chin.

"Where you headed?" he asks.

I tell him the beach.

"Name's Dave," he says. "I can drop you at the causeway."

I don't want to talk, so I look out the window, counting the streets as they tick by, noticing weird things, like the way coconuts clustered at the crowns of palm trees look like faces staring down, or how the Halloween decorations, still hanging from houses and office buildings all along the street, look kind of stupid and out of place this morning.

Dave pulls over just past the light at Blue Heron, and I start to get out.

"Thanks, man," I say.

"Hey," he says, grabbing my arm as I'm opening the door, "whatever it is, it'll be OK, huh?"

I look at him for a minute, thinking, *How the hell can he say it's going to be OK? He can't know what it's like to lose a brother.* Then I realize I don't know anything about him, and my anger fades.

"Thanks," I say. "Thanks for the ride."

There's a pay phone at the corner on the other side of the road. I have to wait for the cars that are coming over from the island and turning onto Federal before I can cross. Finally, there's a break in traffic and I run to the sidewalk on the other side, pick up the receiver of the phone, pop a dime in, and dial. The phone rings twice before anyone picks it up. My heart is beating a thousand miles an hour when a voice comes on.

"Hello?"

"Sally?" I say, and suddenly all of the distances collapse.

Chapter 21

For days now, I've been a zombie. I haven't seen much that's been going on around me. But now, with the sun just beginning to edge above the low clouds that hang along the coast, it's like somebody put a spotlight on the world.

Along the rails of the bridge, some early fishermen hang lines over the side, little bobbers popping up and down. One man is bent over, trying to get a blowfish off his line; the fish is puffed up to the size of two softballs, spikes sticking out in all directions. He's got gloves on and is grabbing at the hook with needle-nose pliers. Underneath the bridge, a small boat grumbles by, heading for the inlet. An old man sits at the wheel, smoking a cigarette and staring absently ahead. The wake from his boat sloshes against the concrete pylons of the bridge.

From the bridge, the walk to the beach takes fifteen minutes. At the corner where I usually turn north up A1A, I stop at a 7-Eleven, go inside, and buy a Coke. I shuffle around for a minute, then push the glass door open and step outside and sit down on the curb in front of the store. Cigarette butts and candy wrappers litter the parking lot; a wadded-up piece of paper skitters across the road from the beach.

"Hey, Jimmy."

I look up to see Sally standing over me. Since Monday, I've just wanted to hide, to be alone. But this morning, especially after finding Dad the way I did last night, I knew I needed to talk to Sally. I owe it to her. I owe it to me. She's my best friend, and I've left her out in the cold.

"Hey," I say. Her eyes are bright and sad at the same time. "Listen, Sally, Frank told me something in his last letter."

"Yeah?" she asks, still standing there, looking down at me.

"Well, he was going to ask Susan to marry him. I don't know if he did or didn't, but she doesn't even know he's gone yet. I haven't been able to call her."

"Wow," she says.

"Yeah, and I'm sure he didn't tell my parents; they

would have just given him a hard time about being too young."

"You should call Susan."

"I know, but what am I going to say? I mean, she'll be a mess."

"But knowing something like this is a responsibility. She's Frank's girlfriend. She's your friend. You owe it to her."

I laugh, but I'm not feeling funny.

"I don't know. . . ."

"You want me to call her?" she asks.

"No, it's something I've got to do."

I stand up, and she puts her arms around me. I start crying again.

"It's OK," she says, pulling me closer. "It's OK."

We stand there for what seems like hours, me feeling hollowed out and broken, her holding me. Her smell fills my head. Her hands feel like sunshine moving across my skin. It's like that first day at the beach with Terry, when Sally and I sort of disappeared into our private world. I'd never felt that way before. And now she's the one person in the world I know I can trust. We've never talked about our feelings for each other. Maybe it's not the kind of thing that words can describe. Maybe it's something you just know and don't ever have to say.

I pull back and just look at her. She puts her hands on either side of my head and pulls my face so close to hers that I can feel the heat radiating from her. And then her lips are touching my lips. Our mouths open and all the words in the world disappear.

When we finally stop to catch our breath, my eyes must be big and stupid-looking, because she starts to laugh.

"You big goof," she says. "Don't look so surprised."

For a second, I forget about everything. I forget about Frank. I forget why I'm here, what Sally and I are supposed to do.

A cop car cruises by but doesn't stop. I grab Sally's hand and say, "Let's get out of here. We don't want to get picked up."

We cross the highway and walk down toward the beach. To make sure the cops won't see us, we walk down to the hard-packed sand along the tide line and head north. For a long time, I don't say anything. Sally's hand is warm in mine; I rub her palm with my finger. She's wearing a white tee-shirt with a yellow oxford shirt over it, and the outer shirt blows back like a sail. Her hair is blowing too.

Up ahead, the dark shape of the *Amaryllis* looms. It looks funny, but I can't figure out what is different. There are smaller boats anchored off the stern, and it looks like men are scrambling around the hull. As we get closer, I see showers of sparks raining down. A crane mounted somewhere inside the rusted body of the ship turns, lifting a huge plate of steel slowly over the side and dropping it just as slowly onto the deck of one of the boats, which I can now see are tugboats. There must be a hundred men in dark overalls, some with helmets and facemasks, swarming over the ship like ants. Welders crouch with torches, cutting away pieces, while other workers wearing yellow hardhats help position and hook the cables from the crane to the pieces that have already fallen away. On the beach, three men in dark suits stand in a circle, pointing up and waving their hands around. One of them is holding a sheaf of papers and seems to be describing something to the others.

We hurry to the cutout in the dune where I had hidden yesterday, the same place we first met. Sally brought a blanket, which she spreads on the sand. I've been running scared; scared of myself, scared of the world, scared of Mom and Dad—scared I'll never see Frank again. Nothing has changed, but for the moment, feeling Sally warm and leaning against me, I feel safe.

We sit for an hour, maybe more, watching the workers disassemble the *Amaryllis*. The heavy throb of diesel engines from the crane and the tugboats is constant. Far out on the horizon a tanker moves north, probably carrying a million gallons of that goopy oil that washes up on the beach in sticky gobs. The same old couple as yesterday walks by, holding hands and laughing.

"Sally," I say, realizing as I speak that it's the first thing I've said since we left the 7-Eleven, "what do you think happens to those guys that get lost in the jungle? I mean, do they torture them? Do they kill them? Do they just stick them in a cell and let them starve?"

She looks out at the lines of waves rolling in, curling over on themselves in frosty crowns of foam.

"I don't know. But I do know there's nothing you can do except to pray for Frank and hope he'll come through it all somehow. Look," she says quickly, pointing up at the sky.

An airplane tugging a long banner chugs slowly along the beach. There is something written on it, but it's hard to read because it's waving back behind the plane. The steady drone of its engine grows louder and pretty soon it's floating there in front of us, the banner stretched out fifty feet behind the tail.

"What does it say?" I'm squinting into the sun and can't quite make it out.

Sally squints, too, but she's able to read the words. "Out of Vietnam Now, Protest Today at John Prince Park," she mouths slowly.

I lean back against the rising slope of the dune. Sally sits back and nestles against me.

"I wonder . . . ," she starts to say, then drifts off, silent.

"What?" I ask. She turns to me, and I can see her eyes are wet.

"Well, I wonder if my brother knows anybody over there, if that would make it different somehow. I mean, a lot of these protesters are mad at the soldiers, but it's not the soldiers' fault we're there. Frank's just another boy like you or my brother. How can they be mad at them?"

I reach and touch her face, drawing my fingers slowly over a tear rolling down her cheek.

"Maybe they've just got to be mad at somebody," I say, "and it doesn't do any good to be mad at the president. But I think they're right to be mad."

We both watch the airplane grow small in the distance. I reach into my pack and pull the letters out.

"I've got something I want to show you," I say, fumbling through the sheets of paper. "These are his. I mean, Frank's letters. I've been reading and rereading them, trying to figure some things out. Even before he disappeared."

She takes them from me and holds them in her lap as if they're Egyptian parchments or something else antique and incredibly valuable. The sounds of work from the ship—diesel engines, banging, and the high-pitched whine of a saw—drift through the air. A gull caws as it flaps overhead. The steady crashing of waves fills all the quiet in between, but it is peaceful, and I know I have to read them to her, one by one, my voice traveling only inches, the real speaker lost somewhere nine thousand miles from here. I reach into the pile and draw one out.

Chapter 22

When I finish reading the first letter, I look up and find Sally staring out at the sea. In one hand, she's clenched a fistful of sand, which is running between her fingers like the sand in an hourglass. Her other hand is curled around her knee, and she's leaning back, pressed against the dune as if some weight is pushing her back.

"Sally?" I say quietly, not understanding.

The work onboard the *Amaryllis* rises in pitch, and I move closer to her.

"You know," she says, still focused on the water, "there's a place in Miami where some guy a bunch of years ago built a castle. He didn't build it, exactly; he bought one in Italy and took it apart. He labeled all the stones and shipped them over here, then put it back together on Biscayne Bay. It's called Viscaya. I've only been there once—my mom and dad took me—but every room is filled with beautiful things. Paintings, old Roman tables, marble bathtubs with gold faucets. It's incredible. I remember walking through that place bored, wishing I could go home and watch TV. But you know, now I wish I could go back and just wander around for days, soaking everything up."

A gull flies overhead, its sharp beak pointed down. The crane swings another huge plate of steel over the side of the ship and lowers it slowly to one of the tugs. Sally buries her head in my shoulder and starts crying.

"How can the same world that made all that beautiful stuff make war in Vietnam?" she whispers, catching her breath and sniffing. "It's not fair."

We sit without moving for the rest of day, reading letters, looking out at the vast sweep of the Atlantic, listening to the noise from the *Amaryllis*. The sun reaches its peak and starts to drop slowly west. Shadows of the sea oats and sea-grape trees stretch longer and longer down the beach. When I finish reading the last one, we stand and brush the sand off our jeans and walk down to the water.

Sometimes, when my mom and dad take me out to dinner, I watch the couples at other tables. It always amazes me to watch a man and woman eat a whole meal without uttering a single word. I've imagined how empty it must feel to be married to someone and have no words left. Now, though, walking on the cool, wet sand, dodging the water as it slides up and then retreats, Sally and I are silent.

But this isn't the uncomfortable emptiness I imagine; it's almost as if we've said so much, shared so many thoughts, that we don't need to talk to know what the other is thinking. Maybe that's what happens to those married couples. It makes me feel a little better to realize that, and I squeeze Sally's hand. She looks at me and smiles. We start to swing our hands between us, and I remember that old couple, laughing and happy.

Sally bumps my shoulder and nestles against me, running her fingers through my hair, a smile creeping across her face. The late afternoon sun casts its slanted light along the slope of the beach. In Sally's eyes, it makes the little stars dance the way it did the first day I met her.

We walk in silence for a while, the steady racket from the *Amaryllis* and the rhythmic cadence of the waves making a kind of music. I guess I thought that after reading Frank's letters all day, we'd be serious and talk about how horrible it all is. But instead, it seems like we have absorbed so much of Frank that there really isn't much left to say. At least there's nothing either one of us could say that would add or subtract anything from what we know about him. I don't think I understand yet what happened over there, but I'm not sure anymore that understanding it matters.

"You know," I say, stopping and turning to Sally, "he's a lot of things to me."

"What do you mean?"

"Well, there's the Frank I remember from home, the Frank I've learned at a distance from his letters—the Frank who I will never really know at all—and the Frank who has disappeared in the jungles of Vietnam. They're all the same Frank, but they're each completely different."

"And there's the Frank I can only know through you," she says. "You carry him and share him, even if he's gone."

Sally and I have walked maybe a mile past the *Amaryllis,* and the sun is beginning to set behind the long line of bushy trees on the other side of the island.

"Maybe we should turn around," she says.

I nod, and we turn and walk back the way we came.

Chapter 23

For the past couple of months, I've been meeting Sally on Singer Island every Saturday and watching as the workers cut the body of the *Amaryllis* away. The days are shorter and cooler now. Not too many people swim, except the snowbirds who fly down here for the winter, driving around in their Cadillacs and flashing money like there's no tomorrow. They're interesting to watch, but I think the demolition of the ship is scaring most of them to other parts of the beach.

There's not much left now but a skeleton rising just above the water line. Each day begins with another train of tugboats lined up. And each day ends with the boats chugging off toward the inlet, heavy in the water with their cargo of salvaged steel. Last week, Sally called and read me an article about the whole thing. They're going to haul what's left offshore and sink it, let it turn into a reef.

Tonight she called in the middle of dinner.

"Jimmy," she said, "they're pulling it off the beach tomorrow."

At the table, Dad is alternately shoveling mashed potatoes into his mouth and sawing at a piece of steak. I watch him as he chews, staring absently out the window at the street. A souped-up GTO burns rubber, then hits the brakes for the stop sign at the corner, all in the space of our block. Dad's eyes are just flat, no emotion. Before, he'd be out there chasing the kid down to get his license plate. And Frank would be muttering to just leave the kid alone. Now Dad just sits and chews.

He hasn't had a drink tonight. In fact, he hasn't had a drink for a month. It's funny. I used to pray to God he'd quit and never touch the stuff again, but now that he's "taking some time off," as he puts it, I almost wish he'd have a drink, just so he'd act like he was alive.

Mom doesn't seem any happier than I am about Dad's change of heart. And that's funny too. Even though in front of me I've never heard her criticize Dad, sometimes when they think I'm asleep I hear them argue about his drinking, and more than once I've heard her tell him if he doesn't stop she'll leave.

After dinner, I clear the table and stack the dishes in

the sink, getting ready to wash them. Dad, who hasn't said a word all night, says, "You're mighty industrious tonight, Junior."

I think he's being sarcastic, and I'm waiting for the other shoe to drop, but when I look up at him, I see he's smiling. I mean a real smile, like he thinks I'm okay. He walks over to where I'm standing and pats his big hands on my back, then turns without saying a thing and goes into the living room.

I dry the plates and glasses and put them in the cupboard, wipe the countertop, and hang the towel to dry. Mom has gone out back and is sitting in the lounge chair.

I call Sally back as soon as the kitchen's clean.

"I'll be there in twenty minutes," I tell her, carefully lifting the car keys from the hook by the telephone as we're talking.

Dad doesn't like me to take the car on school nights, but tonight is special. In my room I stuff Frank's letters, a candle, and some matches in my pack, then I grab a sweater from the closet. Dad is lying on the couch in front of the TV. Mom has come in from the backyard and is doing something in the carport. I open the door and step outside, hoping I can catch her before she comes back in. She's bent over a box in the storage room when I find her.

"Mom," I say, trying to see what she's looking at, "I need to go see Sally. Can I take the car?"

She looks up, holding Frank's graduation picture in her hand. "Sure," she says, "just be back early. You've got school tomorrow."

"What are you doing?"

She doesn't respond, but hands me the picture.

"Mom?" I say, pushing the picture back at her. "Frank's gone, isn't he?"

"I don't know, Jimmy," she says, studying the details of his face.

"He's gone, Mom," I tell her, surprised how sure I am, and how calm. "He's gone and he's never coming back."

She turns to me, tears welling up in her eyes.

"Jimmy," she said, "your dad is a hard man, but what's happened to Frank is not his fault. The world deals us what's coming and that's the end of it."

"I know," I say, opening the door of the car. "I don't blame Dad."

"He loves you, you know?" she says.

"I know."

She stands there, not moving, not saying anything. I start the car and back down the driveway with the lights off so Dad won't see them swinging past the window of the living room. When I get into the street, I turn the lights on, put the car in first, and hit the gas.

Sally's waiting for me at the 7-Eleven. I reach across the seat and push the door open. She hops in, and we head south toward the Rutledge.

There's no one on the beach. It's almost Christmas, and the wind blowing off the ocean is cool. The sky is clear, and I can see a million stars scattered everywhere. We pull into the parking lot of the Rutledge and stop, but I leave the engine running.

"You don't have to do this with me," I say to Sally, holding her hand and watching her face in the weird green light from the dashboard.

"I know I don't have to," she says, "but you'd have to tie me up and gag me to keep me from it."

She's smiling, a kind of sad, serious smile. I get out of the car and close the door. The wind is blowing harder here. The moon, not quite risen yet, lights up the bottom of a stray cloud scudding across the horizon. The dark shape of the butchered *Amaryllis* lies low, waves rolling down its length in long cascades.

We find our carved-out place in the dune, and I put the pack down. I stand there for a minute, looking out at the water. I can't really see the waves, except where the moon lights the crests just as they begin to break.

Sally gets up and walks down to the water's edge. I pick up my pack and open it. I dig around inside until I find the candle and matches. I grab the sheaf of Frank's letters and another single sheet of paper that I'd folded and tucked into my notebook. I put everything but the letters in my pockets and walk down to meet Sally.

We sit a few feet from where the water rushes up and thins and sinks into the sand before pouring itself back into the sea. With my hand I scoop a hollow and stick the candle there, pushing sand up and around it to hold it in place. I put the letters out in front of me and reach into my pocket for the matches. The breeze has almost died, but it's enough that I have trouble lighting the candle. Finally, though, the flame catches and brightens. Sally and I arrange ourselves to block the wind, and the flame steadies. Carefully, I unfold the sheet of paper and hold it up in the flickering light.

Sally has listened to Frank's letters. I've read her all of them, but I feel a little funny now, about to read a letter I've written to Frank, but she touches my arm and looks at me in a way that makes me know it's okay. Far out on the ocean, a freighter sounds the low bellow of its horn. I look back to the paper and the lines I've made in ink. My voice feels funny, like it belongs to someone else, but I push ahead.

Dear Frank,
It won't be long before everyone wakes up,
even in Vietnam. Not too long ago, early in the

morning, before there was even a hint of sun, I heard something outside my window, and I went to look. The grass was wet, the smell of jasmine floated in the night air. I heard a noise, and when I went to look, I found Dad hunched up among the crotons and the dwarf palms, crying. Go figure.

At the time, I thought he'd just been drinking, but it wasn't that. I think for once he got it right. I think for once he understood that you were a part of what made him real in the world. And I think he realized he'd pushed you to the other side of everything he'd ever known and left you there to die. I know you can't forgive him, really, for everything he did. I'm not sure I can. But you're gone now, and I'm still here. I have to find a way to live with him, don't I? Is that what forgiveness is?

I've read and reread the letters you sent to me. I try to hear your voice. I try to remember everything you ever said to me. I guess I don't have much left of you, but at least I have the words you wrote in the jungles of Vietnam, and the memory of you sitting on your board out by the Amaryllis, *waiting for the next wave.*

The moon has risen now above the clouds, casting a path of light across the water. Sally has been sitting beside me this whole time, and now she leans against my shoulder, her hand finding mine, our fingers curling together. I feel tears welling up in my eyes, but I hold them back.

"Jimmy, what if he's not really, you know . . ." She hesitates, the word like something cumbersome and heavy on her tongue. "Dead? I mean . . . he could come home."

I feel her pulse where our hands are touching.

"I know," I say, "but if he's gone, I want to say good-bye. If he comes home, then this is just between you and me."

The night air is cool, even though the breeze has dropped off. The candle is burning bright. I hold the letter in front of me, then touch the edge of the paper to the flame. As it catches and starts to burn, I stand and walk into the water. When there is almost nothing left of the page I let it drop. The last little piece burns for a second, then goes out. The charred remnant floats there in front of me, bobbing up and down, slowly moving seaward with the advancing and retreating swells.

I turn and find that Sally's right behind me. There's nothing to say, the quiet shushing of the waves enough voice for both of us. I bend and swish my hand to wash the black ash of the letter from my fingers, and the water comes alive with a phosphorescent light. I do it again, this time spelling out *FRANK*.

"What makes it do that?" Sally asks.

"It's magic," I say.

"Yeah," she says, and takes my hand as we walk back to where the candle has burned down to the sand.